Romancing Lady Stone

A School of Gallantry Novella

DELILAH MARVELLE

Acknowledgements

The following glorious people have made
this book possible. Big sloppy kisses to
Jessa Slade, Jessie Smith, Máire Claremont,
Deb & Kim Burke, Kim Wollenburg,
Ronnie Buck & Carol Ann MacKay.

To my dearest Reader,

I've never been one to follow a prescribed timeline when it comes to writing a series and *Romancing Lady Stone* is no exception. While, yes, this is a School of Gallantry linked story, its purpose is to deliver a small, unexpected glimpse into the heart beating behind the school itself. Please note that the secondary love story in this novella will have its own full length book in the upcoming Whipping Society Series. So don't panic thinking I left a story untold. This novella does not have to be read with the series. It stands on its own.

Romancing Lady Stone is my cheeky version of star-crossed lovers. Whether you believe in destiny or not, people meet in the most random of places and it leads to the most random of romances. I believe I met my own husband because something otherworldly wanted us to. Our homes were cities apart. We went to different universities. There was no internet at the time and we had no social activities or friends in common that would have ever allowed our paths to cross. The fact that I met my husband on Halloween night was a sure sign of something magical taking place. Seeing it was Halloween, my husband was also dressed as a Russian Military Officer. How the heck could I resist? Given the themes I was playing with, I knew I had to make the hero of this book Russian in honor of my husband. I hope you enjoy getting lost in Russia with Cecilia and learning more about the secret life waltzing behind the walls of the School of Gallantry.

Much love and Happy Reading,

Delilah Marvelle

LESSON ONE

Despite what polite society thinks, a true gentleman is made. Not born.

-The School of Gallantry

Moscow, Russia

Late evening, March 29th 1830

A bone-penetrating glacial breeze whistled in through countless shattered windows, sending snow whirling across a cavernous lobby of a hotel that hadn't seen the bustle of people since Catherine the Great. Cracked marble floors heavily stained by weather and neglect, stretched out into an echoing darkness.

Maybe he was at the wrong address.

Konstantin Alexie Levin paused from his slow stride beside a mold-blackened wall and lowered his chin. A glowing lantern swayed from a rust-crusted hook indicating that someone was, in fact, waiting for him. As instructed.

Stripping off his well-worn leather glove, Konstantin reached out and dabbed a finger against the glass of the lantern. It was still cold to the touch, hinting it had been lit barely moments before his arrival. Pulling his glove back on, he scanned the darkness beyond the dim light. Except for the rustle of dead leaves scraping the floor and the distant roar of the wind lashing snow against the bones of the building, everything else in the blurring darkness was eerily quiet.

Digging into the inner pocket of his heavy winter coat, he dragged out his father's watch and flipped open the silver lid. The click of resisting metal from the latch reverberated as he leaned toward the lantern to better see the hour.

Midnight. How serendipitous.

He snapped the lid shut. Grazing a gloved finger across the fading words etched into the tarnished casing, Konstantin let out a breath that frosted the air and shoved the watch back into his pocket.

Incredibly good things were known to happen to a Levin at midnight. He referred to it as the Glorious Midnight Bane. It had commenced back in 1792, when his father, an upper class gentleman with debts brought on by heavy gambling, had met a beautiful British spinster at the festival of Maslenitsa whilst church bells gonged at midnight. Her name was Miss Penelope Bane.

His father, Mr. Roman Stanislav Levin, had hired an expensive tutor so he could master the British language and then romanced Miss Bane beyond his financial means until the two fell madly in love. In honor of their engagement, his father presented her with an amethyst ring he could not afford and she presented him with a silver pocket watch she could not afford. *'Eternally Yours at Midnight'* was etched on the back of the silver casing in English. Shortly after their betrothal, Miss Penelope Bane tragically died in a horrific carriage accident and was barely identified by the amethyst ring on her finger.

His father, the ultimate romantic, had never recovered and

abandoned the last of his respectable name by becoming part of a powerful criminal organization to avoid going to debtor's prison. He became a different man. But even long after his father married Konstantin's mother, whilst becoming one of the most feared criminals in Saint Petersburg *and* Moscow, he still carried that watch and could often be found sitting with it in silence, opening and closing its silver casing as if communicating with Miss Bane.

Though most would call it superstitious rubbish unworthy of a blink, the repeated connection between the hour and the watch was uncanny. The man only ever conducted business at midnight in honor of Miss Bane, and as a result, had survived everything, each and every time, no matter how outrageous the incident. His father had once travelled with a group of men to an armory where a paid official allowed them to take whatever they needed. It was a quarter to midnight when halfway through their 'shopping' of ammunition, the armory had mysteriously caught fire and blew several walls out of the building. His father was the only one to survive and walked away without a single burn or scratch. The watch was in his pocket.

When Konstantin had fallen deathly ill as a boy, and the doctors could not lower his fever and the priest was brought in, he remembered his father gallantly tucking that watch into his hand and staying with him all night. Whilst other fathers might have given their sons the crucifix during a serious illness, his father gave him the watch. Miraculously, Konstantin had recovered and learned to believe in its power.

And so it was, barely a decade ago, at exactly midnight, his father, his hero, his mentor, who had been battling consumption for months, took his last breath. Miss Bane's watch slipped from that noble hand and fell against the floor beside the bed, shattering the glass casing within. The watch had ceased ticking right along with his father.

Blinded by his own grief during a wake attended by every influential criminal in Russia that offered their condolences (and work), Konstantin had tried to clasp that broken watch into his father's limp hands, but his mother wouldn't permit it. She insisted the watch be pawned. He couldn't do it. He understood his mother had always been sensitive about the subject of Miss Bane, but he also knew what that watch meant to his father. He therefore hid it at the bottom of a drawer. It wasn't until his poor mother died that he had a clockmaker repair the damaged watch. He had carried it in his pocket ever since. It had become an old friend, which protected him and gave him the luck he knew he didn't have.

Much like his father, he never went anywhere without it.

Heavy, booted steps scuffed against the floors of the vast lobby behind him.

Konstantin yanked the dagger from his leather belt and spun toward the sound. He slanted the blade toward the darkness beyond the lantern and called out, "I do not appreciate being summoned to an abandoned hotel as if it were your mother's parlor."

Two men emerged from the shadows and into the dim light. They paused shoulder to shoulder. Expensive, thick fur coats tightly bound their hefty bodies.

"We apologize for inconveniencing you, Mr. Levin," the taller one said. He grinned, exposing crooked but clean teeth. "I am Boris. 'Tis a pleasure to meet you."

"And I am Viktor," the shorter one offered, inclining his head. "We appreciate you meeting us at this hour with the weather being what it is."

Despite their overly warm smiles, Konstantin knew better than to put away the dagger. Midnight may be a lucky hour, but that didn't mean he was stupid.

The one on the left, Viktor, resembled an oil-painted gentleman. From that tonic-drenched blond hair that shone like glass, to a smoothly shaven face. Only vain men insisted on fully shaving their beards during the winter in Russia, because everyone knew facial hair protected the face from all the goddamn wind, ice and snow.

The other one, Boris, looked like most Russians, poor bastard. His dark, shaggy hair touched the large shoulders of his fur coat and his bushy, black beard with its tendrils of grey still held a clump of stew he hadn't properly wiped away from a late supper.

Konstantin gestured toward the man's beard. "You were in a bit of a hurry to get here, I see."

Viktor leaned in and in a quiet tone pointed out the clump of stew to his associate.

Boris hurriedly brushed it out of his beard.

Konstantin lifted a brow. "Your missive indicated this matter was of unmitigated importance." He refrained from tapping his blade against each of their foreheads. "I have no idea who you represent, but I am on the straight path and have been for three full months. I am working alongside a butcher." For measly pay, but it was legal. He was learning a whole new set of skills. "If you have an offer, it had better be respectable and not involve weapons or a fist."

Viktor eyed the blade, then slowly reached into the inner pocket of his fur coat and withdrew a folded parchment. "Should you confuse our visit with your family's sordid past, we wish to assure you we are here on behalf of Duc de Andelot. Forgive the location and the hour but he insisted we call on you outside of prying eyes given the nature of our news. You are being asked not to discuss the details of this meeting with anyone. For your safety."

Konstantin paused. Duc de Andelot? He didn't think he'd ever hear from that one again. Andelot was third cousin to the King of France. Or who had once *been* the King of France. During the storm of the revolution, the duc's face had been heavily marred, forcing him into wearing a black velvet mask. No one had ever seen him without it. Whatever money he'd escaped France with, he had invested heavily into merchant ships sailing into the West Indies.

It made him into the god of gold and power he now was.

The duc had bought a large estate and lived like an aristocratic Russian, even though he was half-French and half-British. Every year, Andelot donated thousands of rubles to the poor, and during harvest, and despite his age of five and sixty, the man stripped down to a linen shirt and trousers, with his mask in place, and went out into the fields with a scythe to muddy his own boots alongside his laborers.

The man was a legend.

Everyone in Moscow revered the duc.

Well...almost everyone.

Three months earlier, Konstantin had been approached by an anti-aristocratic criminal organization to abduct Duc de Andelot and deliver the man into their hands so they could kill him. They believed the duc was a threat to their organization because the peasants liked him too much. What they didn't know was that Konstantin had always secretly admired the duc and that despite bearing his father's well-known name, he, much like his father, wasn't the brute everyone thought he was. Konstantin took the assignment because he was determined to protect Andelot. The night before the appointed abduction, Konstantin was almost killed trying to deliver a secret missive to the duc. Konstantin sustained a bullet to his left shoulder but survived. All of the men involved in the plot to kill Andelot were arrested within six hours and sent to Siberia. The duc, as it turned out, was good friends with the Emperor.

It made Konstantin realize that supporting the violence only created violence. So he retired from the business.

The duc, in vast appreciation, had invited Konstantin into his grand home for a meal and billiards. Not being able to see his face beyond a mask was a touch unnerving, but as the evening went on, Konstantin felt like they were old friends. The duc, in between casual billiard shots, had eventually asked Konstantin what he wanted in return for saving his life. Konstantin asked the man for respectable work so he could become the gentleman his father had once been before criminal life had erased the Levin name. The duc told him he'd be rewarded with something far better. But a day later, the duc had quietly left Russia to go to London to resolve a private matter. That was three months ago.

"I am listening." Konstantin tried not to sound *too* agitated. He hadn't saved the duc's life to be rewarded, but he didn't appreciate being led on, either. "What can I do for him that I haven't already?"

Boris set his mutton-like shoulders. "The stars have decided to shine brightly for you, Mr. Levin."

Konstantin refrained from rolling his eyes. "Metaphors belong to poetry I reserve for beautiful women. Now get to the point. What does he want?"

"The duc has officially declared you one of three beneficiaries to his estate. He made the decision whilst in London. You would not be able to inherit his title, as that privilege passes only from blood to blood, but also, according to France's law of 1808, his title no longer exists amongst the titles Napoleon re-instated. You will therefore only be able to inherit a portion of the funds tied to his name. We were sent to deliver the news to you at an undisclosed location so you were not put into any immediate danger given the amount involved. You are to receive an equal sum of one hundred thousand pounds. Not rubles. Pounds. Unlike the other two names stipulated in his will, your portion of the estate will be delivered into your hands in the next three months. He is, after all, in excellent health and wishes to reward you now, rather than later. You are therefore being mandated to leave Russia and go to London to collect the entire sum."

Konstantin nearly choked on his own spit. One hundred thousand?! Holy— This had to be a joke. It had to be. "And where is your proof that either of you actually represent the duc?" He pointed his five-inch blade toward their faces. "I want to see it."

Viktor hit Boris in the shoulder. "Give him the proof he requires."

Boris puffed out a breath, unfolded his arms and patted his fur coat. From an inner pocket, he withdrew a velvet pouch, which he unstrung. Digging into the pouch with gloved fingers, he removed a gold signet ring with a crest used for legalizing documents. He held it up, angling it toward Konstantin. "His seal. We are sworn to only use it upon his command and destroy it upon his last breath."

Konstantin's eyes widened. It was indeed the duc's seal. He'd seen a similar ring emblazoned on the duc's hand when he dined with the man three months ago. Stunned, Konstantin lowered the dagger. "The duc intends to give me one hundred thousand pounds?"

Boris slid the ring back into its velvet pouch. "Yes."

"Without any stipulations or provisos?"

Viktor nodded. "Yes."

Konstantin pointed the dagger. "*Why?*"

Viktor glanced toward the blade. "Is that necessary, Mr. Levin?"

"Forgive me." Konstantin sheathed the dagger into the scabbard slung around his hip. "I am still transitioning into respectable life."

Viktor promptly held out the parchment he'd taken out earlier. "His Grace asked that we deliver this letter into your hands."

Although good things were known to happen to a Levin at midnight, this was a touch ridiculous. Konstantin tugged the letter from Viktor's gloved hand and turned it over.

Breaking the jet-black wax seal, Konstantin unfolded the parchment and tilted it toward the sliver of light emitted from the lantern hanging beside them. He paused. Similar to the conversation they had shared over a meal and billiards, it was in English.

Mister Levin,

After a long night of getting to know you, which I will admit reminded me of days in my youth spent with old friends who have sadly perished amongst the flames of the revolution, I have concluded you need a more suitable reward for the risk you took in saving my life. My reasoning behind giving you such a large sum goes beyond mere appreciation. Your upbringing has made it difficult for you to erase your past and start anew, which is why I intend to gift you with an opportunity to become the man I know you to be. The one your father and Russia had never allowed you to be. I hope we will continue to be friends. I have very few acquaintances I trust, but you have earned your place amongst those few for life. Please find me at my new home at 32 Belgrave

Square in London. I look forward to seeing you again and apologize for having left Russia so abruptly without sending word. Gratefully,

Duc de Andelot

Jesus. The offer was real.

Pulling out a leather satchel, Boris tossed it at him.

Konstantin caught its weight with a free hand, coins tinkering within.

"It will cover your travelling costs," Boris explained. "Be frugal with it. You will not see anything more until you arrive into England. He suggests taking a boat out of Saint Petersburg by way of the Baltic Sea. It will get you to London faster."

Slowly pushing the satchel into his pocket, Konstantin tightened his hold on the letter. This was actually happening to him. He was going to be disgustingly wealthy. He'd earned thousands merely by doing the right thing. Imagine that.

Lowering his gaze to the letter, he let out the breath he didn't realize he was holding. No more trying to cover the holes in his boots with polish. No more drinking vodka that might make him blind. No more cleaver swinging at a butcher shop and inhaling acrid meat for mere rubles a week in order to get respect. Life was going to be whatever he imagined. With a hundred thousand, the possibilities were limitless.

He'd always wanted to go to London.

Just for the women alone.

Much like his father, he had become obsessed with British women and had often watched them coming in and out of the expensive hotels in Moscow as they pertly bustled from shop to shop under lace parasols. They were educated, knew how to speak fluent French and smelled divinely of expensive perfume whenever they breezed past in those well-corseted hips that swayed in the latest fashion. They lacked the pretentious formality of the Russian ladies.

Of course, women of such caliber never noticed men like him. It made for a rather pathetic life of him watching and never touching. Sadly, the last time he'd even attempted to engage *any* woman of *any* caliber was almost a year ago. He had met her during a theatrical performance he had attended. The woman was beautiful, intelligent and…married. He didn't know she was married until *after* he'd had sex with her in a hotel room she had rented for them. He should have known better. He'd forgotten to wear his watch that night. Not even an hour later, her husband showed up at the hotel door with four other men and whilst two held him, the rest took turns beating the blood out of him until he lost consciousness.

He didn't blame the husband at all. But he'd stayed away from women since. He figured he would live longer.

Folding the parchment, Konstantin tucked it deep into his pocket. He still didn't want to believe it. "Whilst I genuinely question the duc's sanity, tell him I am beyond grateful and will travel to London at once."

Boris dug out a calling card from his fur coat. He flicked it out, holding it between two thick fingers. "Should you have any other questions or concerns before leaving Moscow, please call on us in a manner that would not bring attention to your circumstance."

Konstantin took the card. "Thank you."

"We will inform the duc of your response by courier. A good-evening to you, Mr. Levin." Both men smiled, inclined their heads and turned. Their heavy footfalls echoed on their way out before disappearing out into the wind and snow.

Silence reigned again in the abandoned building.

Konstantin exhaled a frosty breath, letting tension seep out from his chest. It was the strangest midnight he'd ever known. And something told him, this was just the beginning.

LESSON TWO

Adventure is good for the soul. Most of the time.

-The School of Gallantry

Somewhere in Russia

Weeks later

A warm male hand smoothed away her pinned curls from her forehead and tucked her better against the curve of his arm and lap. The tips of his calloused fingers gently skimmed her cheeks and then her nose before resting on the curve of her chin. His lingering touch promised more than unending pleasure. It promised a lifetime of all things beautiful and romantic. It was pulse-rending. It was genuine. It was divine.

She didn't want to wake up.

But of course she did.

Lady Cecilia Evangeline Stone was startled out of a deep slumber when she was jostled against the cushioned seat of the travelling coach. A strange haze edged into her vision, blurring the shadows of the night with the golden halo of a lantern that dimly illuminated the small, upholstered space. It was so odd, but everything swayed more than the actual carriage.

She froze, realizing her cheek and pinned hair, was pressed against a trouser-clad muscled thigh and that a long, masculine arm was heavily draped around her waist. It was a male thigh and a male arm she had never remembered meeting or inviting into her life.

Unable to breathe against the soft scent of charred wood and soap drifting from his clothing, she scrambled up and out of that lap and shoved his arm away. Stumbling toward the far end of the seat, she tightened the cashmere shawl around her cloak, gown and shoulders, unable to make sense of what was happening.

A young, good-looking man, who clearly hadn't shaved in days, intently searched her face from where he sat beside her. His black hair was scattered beneath a low-slung cap that shadowed the color of his eyes. His rugged intensity softened as his glance slid to her décolletage before lifting again. He inclined his head as if hopeful of an introduction.

She gaped. Who was he? And what was he doing in her carriage? Scanning the empty seats surrounding them, which were dimly lit by the coach lanterns, she stilled. This was not her carriage. The upholstery was old, ragged and barely clung to the walls and ceiling.

Her heart skid to a frenzied halt as she glanced toward the empty, frayed seats and the mud spattered windows that framed a black, starless night and a rapidly moving road and open fields. Dearest God. Where was her translator and travelling companion? "Mrs. Bogdanovich?" she called out in disbelief, as if the woman were hidden somewhere within the upholstery.

Cecilia pressed a trembling hand against her mouth to keep herself from screaming as panic flared through every inch of her.

The carriage jerked.

She stumbled, almost falling off the seat.

Large bare hands jumped toward her and grabbed her corseted waist. The man steadied her, pulling her back onto the seat beside him. Well-muscled arms shifted against her from beneath his travelling coat as the hilt of a large dagger attached to a sizable leather belt grazed her thigh and skirts. His hands casually slid up her back, adjusting her against his side and the seat.

With a solid push of panicked hands, she broke his hold on her.

He held up both hands to demonstrate that he had no intention on harming her. Despite the fact he wore a distinguished, pinstriped waistcoat beneath a wool coat of respectable means, there was no cravat around that neck and his linen shirt was scandalously left open, exposing a masculine throat and the upper portion of a broad, well-muscled chest that had clearly seen too many hours of labor.

Cecilia tried not to awkwardly gape at his exposed chest. "Do you speak English, sir?"

Enigmatic eyes, whose color she still couldn't make out in the shadows, met hers from beneath the rim of his wool cap. He lowered his hands and to her complete astonishment, he offered in well-educated English, "I do. Were you looking for conversation?" His low, husky voice was surprisingly sophisticated and laced with a heavy Russian accent that penetrated not only the walls of the carriage but every inch of her skin.

It was like she had never heard a man speak before. It was unbelievably sensuous and made her feel as if he was thinking about doing things to her. Her throat tightened. "Were you touching me whilst I slept?"

He shifted his jaw, a teasing gleam flickering in his eyes. "Not in that way. I prefer my women to remember what I do."

She pressed herself to the opposite side of the seat, setting as much distance between them. She couldn't breathe knowing she was alone with some Russian wielding a dagger and that her travelling companion was somewhere back in the last village. Or the last three villages, for all she knew.

She had to speak to the driver.

Frantically snatching up her reticule from the seat beside her, Cecilia turned and thwacked the glass window several times. "Driver?" she called out as loud as she could. "Stop the coach, please. *Stop the coach*!"

A large calloused hand grabbed her wrist, stilling her hand and reticule from hitting the window again. "Ey." He leaned in closer in reprimand, revealing the sharpening green of his eyes. "What are you doing? I have a schedule to keep."

Between uneven breaths, Cecilia clutched her beaded reticule higher between them with a trembling hand, signaling to him that she was ready to bash his brains out with every last bead in its stitch. "If you touch me again, sir, I will hurt you and your schedule. I am trying to speak to the driver. Now let go of me!" She shook her reticule toward him for good measure.

Those green eyes brightened. He released her wrist. "How charming. You wish to threaten my life with a reticule." He leaned in and lowered his voice dramatically. For effect. "If you put a few rocks in it, *dorogaya moya*, I guarantee it will work much better."

He removed his cap, causing his dark hair to cascade onto his forehead. "I doubt the driver speaks any English. Few people in Russia do. Only the upper classes know the language. Fortunately for you, my father taught me how to speak it incredibly well. He had often told me, if it were not for my Russian accent and my incredible good looks, I could have easily been British." He smiled. "Can I be of service to you?"

This one thought he had a sense of humor. She lowered her reticule back into her lap, trying to focus and stay calm. "Is this your carriage?"

"No." Leaning back against the seat, he flicked the peeling upholstery with a bare finger. "I can assure you, I have far better taste than this." He tilted his head toward her. "This is a public stagecoach. Did you not know that when you paid your fare?"

Her eyes widened. How had she ended up on a public stagecoach? Where was the carriage she had originally hired?

He paused. "Is something wrong?"

"Yes!" She gestured frantically toward the empty seat across from them. "My travelling companion is-is…missing! Have you seen her? And do you know how I got to be here? Because I…I don't remember." She tried to keep her voice calm lest she fall into hysterics.

The carriage jostled against the uneven grooves of the muddy road before settling into an even, swaying rhythm.

He shifted toward her. "How can you not remember?" His brows came together. "You were already on this stagecoach when I boarded hours ago."

She blinked. "*Hours ago*? Was anyone with me?"

"No. Not when I boarded."

She almost fainted. What had happened to Mrs. Bogdanovich? And why couldn't she remember getting into the coach after her meal at the inn?

"You slept the whole while and kept nestling into my lap no matter what I did." He patted his thigh to demonstrate where she had rested. "I eventually stopped moving you off my lap and simply made certain you did not fall off the seat."

Her lips parted. She had *nestled* into his lap? That certainly explained why he'd been touching her. She had left him with very little choice. "Forgive me, sir. I didn't mean to impose or accuse you of anything inappropriate."

He shrugged. "I have been accused of worse. And it was hardly an imposition. You appeared exhausted." He sounded sincere.

Cecilia set a disbelieving hand against her throat, feeling as if they had already shared a very intimate moment she couldn't even remember. "Apparently, the mint *kvass* I drank back at the inn was strong. Very strong. I don't remember anything." Except for his hands.

"I take it you have very thin blood?" he asked.

"Thin— Whatever do you mean?"

He hesitated. "*Kvass* has very little alcohol. You do know that, yes?"

She squinted. That made no sense. If it had very little alcohol, why had it affected her so? Something wasn't right. "What time is it, sir? Do you know?"

He dug into his inner pocket and withdrew a watch attached to a chain. Flipping open the tarnished silver lid that had several notable dents in its surface, he tilted it toward the light of the lantern shining in. He stared at the watch, his expressive, rugged face stilling.

Something was clearly wrong. "Sir? What is it? Is the hour not showing?"

He slowly veered his gaze to hers. "Ah…no. It is showing. It always shows." He cleared his throat, playing with the weight of the watch against his hand. "The hour is midnight. On the tick."

Midnight? She had been sleeping since three in the afternoon? How was that even possible? Three o'clock had been the time she and Mrs. Bogdanovich had stopped at one of the inns for a meal. Why couldn't she remember anything beyond that? Cecilia blinked down at her bare hands still clutching her reticule. Had she not been wearing gloves?

He snapped the lid shut, making her look up.

She had to do something. She had to do something before she ended up on the other side of the continent. "Forgive me, sir, but I'm going to have to stop the coach. I have to go back to Strelna. It's the last city I remember being in."

"You cannot be serious." He slipped his watch and chain back into his coat with a thumb. "Strelna is ten hours away."

Cecilia centered her breath. "My son is getting married against my will, and I'm alone in Russia and don't speak the language. Mrs. Bogdanovich is my translator and travelling companion, and the fact that she is missing concerns me. Greatly. What if something happened to her?"

His features tightened. "Let us pray nothing has." He leaned toward her. "Might I be of assistance? What do you need?"

She wanted to grab that unshaven face and kiss him for gallantly offering help. A breath escaped her. "Can you tell the driver to turn this coach around and go back to Strelna?"

He stared. "I can. But I am only a half hour from my stop and Strelna is ten hours away."

Oh. That would be rather rude, wouldn't it? "Forgive me. I will ensure you find your stop first." Cecilia softened her voice. "In the meantime, could you please open the window and speak to the driver? Surely he would know how I got to be here and what happened to my travelling companion. I do not speak any Russian, sir, and therefore will require your assistance in this. Please."

"I am at your service." He tossed his hat onto the seat before them. "Give me a moment." He rose to an imposing height of over six feet and bent his head and shoulders against the low ceiling of the carriage.

Glancing back at her, he unlatched the window with a quick sweep of his hand. With the dip of a broad shoulder, he leaned out the window and hollered something, his dark hair lifting and scattering against the wind that roared into the space of the coach.

The driver hollered something back over the thundering clatter of wheels.

The man paused and glanced back at Cecilia, his brows coming together. He hesitated, his rugged features hardening. Leaning further out, he gruffly shouted something else, his tone now feral and nothing like the tone he had offered her.

She swallowed. What was going on?

The driver yelled a whole flurry of words as if the world were coming to an end.

Hitting the top of the outside carriage with a quick fist that thudded the roof, the man boomed something to the driver in reprimand.

The driver yelled another long flurry of words.

Leaning back in, the man latched the window, quieting the space again and shook his head. "*Dolbo yeb.*" He settled his large frame into the cushion beside her, causing the seat to sink. Swiping long strands of dark hair from his face, he crossed the ankle of a mud-crusted boot over his knee and scratched at his unshaven chin. "We have a little problem, *dorogaya moya.*"

His tone indicated the problem was anything but little. She almost grabbed him. "What? What did he say? What is it? What happened?"

"He was paid to take you."

Dread seized her. "Paid? What do you mean?"

He dropped his hand onto his thigh. "According to him, you were delivered unconscious to his coach by two men outside a tourist inn back in Strelna. Do you not remember anything?"

Her eyes burned. "Two men?" What had she been doing with two men? "That isn't possible. I…I wasn't travelling with any men. I don't even remember *meeting* any men."

He swiped his face. "They told him you had a medical condition. He was paid to drop you off three towns from the next stop so your brother could take you to the doctor."

She gasped. "*My brother*? I have no brother. Nor do I have a medical condition!"

He intently scanned her gown. "Are you sore in any unusual places?"

Her pulse thundered. "Are you insinuating these men might have…?"

"Yes." He was quiet for a moment. "Should we take you to a doctor?"

Cecilia almost retched at the thought. But fortunately, no. Aside from the dizziness that had already waned, everything below the waist felt normal. As normal for a woman who hadn't had sex in seven years. "No. That isn't necessary." She pressed a hand to her stomacher, trying to keep herself and her voice calm.

"Are you certain?"

Her face burned. "I appreciate your concern, but everything feels as it should."

He puffed out a breath. "You are incredibly fortunate."

Is that what he called it? "I don't consider my situation fortunate at all. Dearest Lord, *I don't even know where I am*!"

"Try to remain calm." He held out a coaxing hand. "The driver will be attaching new horses in less than a half hour. You will get off with me. I will help you."

Her lips parted. "Get off with you? But I don't even know you."

"You need help. And I will help you. You cannot trust the driver or anything he says. Most of these drivers in between main cities get paid to do things they should not. You are getting off with me. Do you understand? Your safety calls for it."

Could she trust him? *Should* she trust him? "What about Mrs. Bogdanovich?"

"What about her?"

"I have to go back to Strelna and find her. What if these men did something to her?"

He glanced toward the latched window. "From what I remember of the schedule, another coach heads back toward the direction of Strelna in eight days. Unfortunately, we will not be able to get to her sooner. The warm weather has melted the snow and made travel slow. The roads are very muddy."

Cecilia sat up. "*Eight days*? I cannot strand her for that long. I'm carrying all of our money. Please. Tell the driver I will pay him a hundred rubles to change out the horses at the next stop and turn this coach around." She loosened the string on her reticule and dug into it, trying to find money to count out for the driver. "Tell him I have more than enough to—" She paused, swatting the emptiness of the silk inside. Where was her money? And more importantly, what had happened to her son's letter? The one with the address where she was supposed to call on him once she got to Saint Petersburg?

She looked up, her fingers savagely tightening against her reticule. "Where is my money? And where is the letter that was with it? Did you take it?"

He leaned back, his rugged features tightening. "You may not want to insult your savior."

Savior? That was a bit much. "You are the only man sitting in this coach with me," she pointed out raggedly. "What else am I to think, sir? I cannot readily verify what you and the driver did or did not say. For all I know you and he are orchestrating this."

"Have you considered that these two men who paid the driver might have emptied your reticule long before I boarded?"

"And why would they have left it behind? They could have made good money off the reticule alone." She shook it. "It was stitched and beaded in Paris."

He swiped his mouth in an attempt to hide a smirk behind a large, ungloved hand. "Oh, yes. Every man in Russia looks for reticules stitched and beaded in Paris."

She glared. "I am stranded and have been robbed, sir. And you dare amuse yourself with my situation?"

"I can assure you, it is not your situation I am amused by." He leaned far back and slowly held open both sides of his coat, exposing the pinstriped waistcoat that made his broad chest look even broader. "Search me. I insist."

Feeling her body heat and ripple at the bold invitation, she shot him an exasperated look. "I am not touching you."

"I am trying to set your mind at ease and get you to trust me. Now search me." He held his coat open wider. "I have pockets in my trousers, too."

She refused to look at those pockets or those trousers. "I am fine with assuming you don't have it."

He released his coat. "You mentioned your son. Did he want you coming into Russia? Would he have arranged for this?"

Heavens above what sort of people was he used to dealing with? John would *never* ambush his own mother. He was a good boy. Most of the time. "No. He would never. He and I are very close and get along very well." As long as she and John didn't get on the subject of his women. "He is marrying a Russian actress." And the worst of it? All of her friends looked at her as if *she* had somehow put the idea into her son's head. Only her daughters thought the whole affair to be incredibly exciting and romantic. Which was why she left them back in London with the governess. Lest any of her daughters get fanciful ideas and start marrying their own set of Russians actors well before they turned eighteen.

He let out a low whistle. "A Russian actress? I wish to offer him many blessings and congratulations."

Cecilia held up a hand. "I ask that you please not offer either. I am actually going to stop the wedding. Whilst an actress is hardly something a mother ought to boast about, in truth, it's the least of my worries. I genuinely wanted to support it, given my son claims to be in love with her, but she is twenty-four years older than him and he is heir to a very large estate. He *has* to have children."

"Ah." He tilted his head. "I am now rather curious. Which actress is he supposed to marry? I may know the name. I attend theatre performances all the time."

She blinked. He hardly seemed the sort to attend theatrical performances. But then who was she to judge? "Her name is Mrs. *Kat...er...ino...chkin.* Did I say that right?"

"*Katerinochkin?*" He coughed out a rough laugh and winced. "Allow me to pray for your son's soul whilst he still has one."

She pulled in her chin. "What do you mean? Do you know her?"

He rolled his eyes. "No. She is simply a very well known actress coming to the end of her popularity. I saw her perform last year when she came into Moscow. She is known for bleeding men dry." Using a forefinger to replicate a pistol, he pointed it to his head and flicked down his thumb. "Her last lover put a bullet through his head upon discovering she had emptied his pockets down to the lint before moving on to another man. It was all over the papers."

Papers that her son apparently did not read. Oh Lord. She didn't need this. And most certainly not now. "I have to get to my son. I knew this woman was taking advantage of him. He is far too young to marry and has always been incredibly shy around women."

"If he is involved with an actress he is shy no more." He grunted. "How old is he?"

"One and twenty."

He pointed at her. "Save him."

"I plan to."

"Good." Dropping his foot back to the floor with a thud, he reached out and dragged her empty reticule toward himself. Turning it upside down, he shook it once, to verify that it was in fact empty. With the flick of a wrist, he tossed the reticule onto the seat across from them. "I do not wish to add to your panic, but I am beginning to think this Bogdanovich of yours, whom you were travelling with, robbed you. That would explain why she is not with you. Did you have any trunks? Because there were none attached to the coach when I boarded."

Her lips parted. No. No, no, no. She shook her head, refusing to believe it. "That isn't possible. Mrs. Bogdanovich is a respectable woman. One I have gotten to know quite well. She came into Russia with me from

England. She also has our travelling papers and—" A gasp escaped her. How was she going to leave the country without papers?

He paused. "The *kvass* you drank. You mentioned it was strong. It should not have been. Who gave it to you?"

Oh, no. "Mrs. Bogdanovich."

"After you drank it, what happened?" he pressed.

Oh, no. "I could barely stay awake. She insisted we retire instead of travelling on and assisted me into a room that was blurring. So I..." She was so stupid. "I don't remember anything after that." She knew that *kvass* didn't taste right. It had been overly bitter. And she drank the whole thing!

He puffed out a breath. "Drugging tourists during a meal is commonplace in Russia. Once a tourist is unconscious, swindlers take everything, put them on a coach and pay a driver to deposit them hours away so no one knows about it."

This couldn't be happening. "But the woman came highly recommended to me."

"By who?"

"A friend of mine."

"Consider them your friend no more. How much money did you travel with? Did this woman know about it?"

She wanted to cry. "Yes. She knew I had brought three thousand."

"*Three thousand?*" he echoed, straightening. "You should *never* travel with that sort of money. Never." He muttered something in Russian and then said, "She was probably working with others. Possibly her family. Which would explain the two men who delivered you to the coach. She could not have done it all on her own."

She paused. "You certainly know quite a lot about these things."

He was quiet for a moment. "I have seen a lot. More than a man should."

She refrained from hitting her head against the window of the carriage beside her. "What am I going to do? I have no money, no clothes and no idea where I'm even at!"

"Where are you going? What is your final destination?"

She was officially dependant on a complete stranger. "Saint Petersburg." She turned toward him, her dark skirts bundling against the seat between them. "How many days away am I? Do you know? Am I on the right coach?"

He intently searched her face.

Cecilia stared back. "Please don't tell me I'm on a coach to Siberia."

He rumbled out a laugh. "No." He rubbed his chin. "If you get off at the next stop, you will only be seven hours away from Saint Petersburg. Coincidentally, I am heading there myself to catch a boat on the Baltic." He dropped his hand onto his knee. "Allow me to pay for your connecting coach into Saint Petersburg."

Astounded by his generosity, she leaned in. "I wouldn't be imposing?"

His gaze held hers. "No. Not at all."

Why was he staring? "Thank you."

His voice grew husky. "Of course."

She tried not to let the raw huskiness of that voice trace her spine. Though she wanted to be at ease knowing she was fortunate enough to have transportation to Saint Petersburg, she now had a much bigger problem. How was she going to find her son without an address or a street name? "Sir? How well do you know Saint Petersburg?"

His gaze remained riveted to her face. "I was born and raised there prior to moving to Moscow a few years ago. Why?"

A breath escaped her. He knew English and Russian and knew the city of Saint Petersburg. He was a Godsend. "Forgive me for even asking, but would you consider assisting me locate my son once we get into Saint Petersburg? I know nothing about the city or the language and have no idea how I am to find him."

He sat straighter. "Where in Saint Petersburg are you going? What street is he on?"

She bit her lip hard. Her son's letter, which had been in her reticule, bore the address, which sadly, she couldn't remember. She had only glanced at it only once or twice. The street name was...Ga... something. Or was it Gor...something? Either way, it was hardly helpful. "My son bought a home. I don't remember the street name or the address, as it was quite recent, but he wrote in his last letter that it overlooked the Neva River on the east side. Do you know where the river is? Maybe we can find him that way."

He lowered his chin. "Do you know how big the Neva is? 'Tis over fifty miles long. We would be better off standing in the street yelling out his name."

Her mouth went dry. She was lost. In Russia.

He eyed her. "Are you married?"

She pulled in her chin. "What does that have to do with anything?"

He adjusted his dagger at his waist. "Because I wish to know what I can and cannot do with you."

Cecilia leaned away from him *and* that dagger. "Begging your pardon, but you are not doing *anything* with me."

"You misunderstand. You have a son and appear to be respectable, therefore you must have a husband. Is your husband in Saint Petersburg with your son? Because I have no wish for misunderstandings. I have had my share of it and husbands can be needlessly aggressive."

She blinked. Oh. "No. You needn't worry about— My husband passed away. Seven years ago." It was so odd to say it aloud. She rarely thought about Frederick anymore and felt incredibly guilty knowing it.

He dropped his hand to his side. "So you have no man?"

The way he said it made her think he was about to volunteer to be that man. "No."

He hesitated and searched her face. "How old are you?"

She blinked. Was he flirting with her? *Now*? Knowing she was in a state of panic and lost in the bowels of Russia? "Surely, you jest. I am old enough to be your mother."

His features stilled. "My mother is no longer alive. So do not speak of her."

Her heart squeezed. "Oh. Forgive me. I didn't mean to…"

Turning to the small, mud spattered window beside him, he propped his head against the glass. "She was very ill. She suffered."

Now she felt like a complete dolt. She softened her voice. "In answer to your question, sir, I am forty."

"Are you?" He veered his gaze back to her. "I am a full thirty." He said it as if to impress her. Lifting his head from off the window, he leaned toward her and draped an arm against his own knee. His eyes boldly raked over her. "You are incredibly beautiful."

She almost sank deeper into the seat. Were all Russians like this? His casualness toward her was unnerving. She was a titled widow with four children.

"The name is Konstantin Alexie Levin." He inclined his head, holding her gaze.

Why did she suddenly feel like fanning herself? "'Tis a pleasure to meet you, Mr. Levin."

He still held her gaze. "Is it?"

Now she *really* felt like fanning herself. "I can assure you it is."

"Might I ask for a name? Since we are officially travelling together?"

"I am Lady Stone."

"Lady?" He raised himself off his knee. "You mean to say you are of British aristocracy?"

"Yes."

He draped a long, muscled arm across the back of the upholstered seat, straining his coat against the movement. "Did you think travelling with another woman was a good idea?" It was obvious by his gruff tone he wasn't looking for an answer, but was actually issuing a reprimand. "A lady of your standing ought to be travelling with a man. And guards. Because another woman can do nothing to protect you. *Nothing*."

She blinked rapidly and edged away, feeling her skin prick beneath that penetrating gaze. He clearly did not understand the underpinnings of British society. Or that she would rather be robbed all over again than to have had her own cousin, Lord Gunther, travel alongside her. "Hiring a female companion is what respectable women of my circle do when they travel, Mr. Levin. I have no male relatives I would willingly travel with and a male companion outside of one's family insinuates indecency. Which is why I hired Mrs. Bogdanovich."

He slowly shook his head from side to side. "Here in Russia, where land is vast and the people are desperate, such respectable thinking ends badly. Most robberies in Russia result in death. Why? Because the majority of swindlers have *no* understanding as to how much laudanum goes into a cup. Given how deeply and how long you slept, I have no doubt if you had been given a touch more laudanum, you would have been dead. You *should* have been dead if Strelna was where you were drugged. Because that means you have slept for over ten hours."

She swallowed knowing he was right. She would have been dead without having ever gotten around to seeing her daughters or her son properly marry. She would have been dead before she could hold her grandchildren or travel to Paris and breathe in the sort of wild adventure she had always yearned for. She had once read in the gossip papers that Parisian women waltzed naked with their lovers in the privacy of their flats and smoked cheroots in public. Secretly, she had always wanted to try both.

Mr. Levin leaned back against the seat. "Fortunately for you, Lady Stone, your son is associating with a well-known actress, which will make it easy to find him. All we have to do is inquire at the theatre she performs in when we get into Saint Petersburg. Depending on how well that goes, you should be with your son in two days. Three at most."

She almost slumped back against the seat. She had never been more thankful. "Your kindness has no bounds."

"Let us not exaggerate. It has its bounds."

She bit back a smile. She liked him. He didn't pretend to be anything more than what he was. She envied people who didn't have to lead their lives according to a title. Unlike her, they could waltz naked with a cigar. "I cannot thank you enough. Is there anything I can offer you in return for the assistance you are providing?"

He extended his long, trouser-clad leg and let his worn, leather boot hit the upholstered seat across from them. Flakes of dried mud spattered the seat. "A beautiful woman should *never* ask a man what he really wants." His green eyes studied her and his mouth quirked. "He may tell you."

Her pulse fluttered knowing he was flirting with her. She tightened her hold on her shawl. "You certainly are anything but coy, Mr. Levin," she countered.

He dropped his leg from the seat and took back his arm from the seat. His eyes brightened as he shifted toward her. "Being coy never got me anywhere."

She locked her knees together. "My son will pay you when we find him," she offered, trying to change the course of their conversation. "I will ensure it is generous."

"I would never take anything for assisting a woman." He leaned in across the seat, that charred, smoky scent of wood drifting in from the heat of his body. "Even if there was something I wanted."

Unspoken words of 'Which there is' hung between them.

She felt her entire body ripple in awareness. She leaned back, her shoulder bumping into the wall of the carriage behind her.

He smirked. "You are not as bold as you paint yourself, Lady Stone, are you?" Drawing in closer, he brushed a hand over her shoulder, lowering his gaze to his fingers that traced an area of her cashmere shawl. "Sadly, there appears to be some damage to your shawl. A part of it is unraveling."

She swallowed, feeling faint from the tips of her ungloved fingers down to the tips of her toes buried in her stockings and half boots. Her shawl wasn't the only thing unraveling. For some reason, she now envisioned him shredding apart her clothing at the stitch with bare hands and whispering words in Russian to her until she herself spoke Russian. Her heart lurched, her breath coming in uneven takes. It was amazing how being away from her three girls had suddenly turned her into a woman. Not a mother. A woman. She had honestly forgotten what that was.

Almost dying apparently did something to a woman's mind.

He took back his hand. "Forgive me. I should not have touched you." Rising from the seat, he turned and fell back into the seat across from hers. His sharp features dimmed. He dragged out his watch and flipping it to the backside of the silver casing he slid a finger across what appeared to be etched words. He tucked it back into his waistcoat pocket and shifted his unshaven jaw, watching her.

Despite the coolness of the air in the carriage, her palms grew moist. The man made her want to do things she thought she'd long outgrown. Because, holy heaven, he was everything her husband had never been. Young, good-looking, dashing and outspoken.

She'd been married almost fourteen years to the day when her husband, Frederick, had died back in 1823, which was now seven years ago. Lord Stone had gone to sleep one night in his room and had never woken up. Despite the fact that she had grudgingly learned to love him in her own way, she lived every day of those fourteen years knowing she had married him for his money and that he had married her for her youth and her beauty.

It didn't make for a good marriage.

Sex was scheduled. It occurred every Monday and Friday evening. If the man wasn't busy or tired. Sometimes, she climaxed, but only when and if he put effort into it. All too many times, she learned to lay on her back, thinking about nothing in particular until he was done. He would then roll off, pat her cheek in thanks, shrug on his robe and plod back to his room. He never embraced her after the act. Nor did he ever stay in her bed to sleep. He thought it was in poor taste for a man to display any form of affection, even behind closed doors. She quickly mastered the art of using her fingers and would wantonly imagine she was being ravaged by one of her good-looking male neighbors.

Though Frederick travelled extensively prior to their marriage, he never held any interest in letting her or the children see much of the world. Going up into Scotland was considered worldwide travelling for their family. His sole interest had been collecting antiquities, attending parliament sessions during debates and taking long walks. Alone. Always alone. He spent time with her and the children only when it suited him. Which wasn't often.

He did, however, let her buy whatever she wanted. In fact, he encouraged it because it was his way of making up for being so morbidly removed. She therefore spent a lot of time shopping with her children and together they always delivered bountiful weekly boxes of items to countless charities throughout London. It made for a rather uneventful life spent solely in shops and…well, shops.

Such was the bane of marrying a man for money. One had everything yet nothing.

Adjusting his coat, Mr. Levin smoothed out the fabric of his trousers against his knee and flicked his gaze to the window. "We are slowing. Are you getting off with me?"

"I most certainly won't be travelling on to find out who my 'brother with the doctor' is," she chided.

He smirked. "'Tis good to know you have a sense of humor about this."

She sighed. "Panicking certainly never served me well."

"It never serves anyone well. Chin up. We will find your son."

The driver called out something in Russian and the carriage

slowed, tugged and pulled until it clattered to a complete halt.

Silence now pulsed around them.

Mr. Levin swiped up his wool cap from the frayed upholstered seat, tugged it onto his head and grabbed up her reticule, shoving into his coat pocket. Opening the door with his shoulder and weight until it swung out, he jumped down from the coach with a resounding thud of leather boots crunching into gravel, turned and snapped out a large hand. "Our connecting coach into Saint Petersburg does not arrive for another two days. There is a small inn down the road. You and I can share a room until the coach comes in. I will pay for it."

She tightened her hold on her shawl at the thought of sharing a room for two nights with a good-looking Russian she just met. In all her forty years, she had never strayed. As a mother to four children, she had gone above and beyond ensuring no man, especially her cousin, stepped anywhere near their lives after the death of her husband. Her children came first. And even though she *had* considered taking a lover, for she did get lonely, she had this irrational fear her children would somehow pick the lock at night and walk in on her doing things with men she shouldn't.

Her fingers dug into the softness of her cashmere shawl. If she didn't ask for a separate room she *knew* she would end up doing things with him. Because those green eyes made her want to shove him against a wall and show him how dangerous a deprived woman could be. "Might I ask for a separate room, Mr. Levin?"

He shifted from boot to boot, still holding out his hand. "I would offer, but my funds are limited until I get to London."

She gaped. So much for escaping him. "London? Why are you going to London?"

He paused. "I plan to live there for a small while until I decide what to do next. Why do you ask?"

What if people found out about their association and that she had shared a room with him in Russia? Regardless of what did or did not happen, she'd be lynched by all of society. And her daughters, who were a tender thirteen, fifteen and sixteen, would never see the respectable debuts they deserved. She couldn't breathe. "Mr. Levin. I live in London."

"Do you?" He sounded as pleased as he was surprised. He shifted closer, his travelling coat opening wider. "How do you like it there?"

He clearly didn't understand. "I am asking for a separate room. Please."

He dropped his hand to his side. "As much as I would like to oblige, Lady Stone, I cannot afford two separate rooms for two nights. I barely have enough to get me into England and I still have to purchase food for you and myself over these next two days *and* buy us fares into Saint Petersburg." He leaned forward and draped an arm against the open door of the coach. "I can give you the room whilst I sleep in the corridor at night. Would that be acceptable?"

She wasn't about to let him pay for the room and then have him sleep in the corridor. Oh, dear. "There is no need for you to sleep in the corridor on my account. You and I will manage." Somehow. "All I ask is that you not speak of this to anyone whilst in London."

"I will tell no one. I consider myself to be a gentleman." Pushing away from the door, he held out his hand again. "Allow me to assist you from the coach."

He certainly did appear to be a gentleman. It was astonishing. A woman would never know it given his lack of cravat, the size of that dagger and his unshaven face. "Thank you, Mr. Levin." She rose, gathering her skirts from around her booted feet and lowered her head through the opening of the coach.

He grabbed her hand, his rough heat penetrating the coolness of her skin. He paused, his fingers skimming her inner palm. "Your hand is cold."

"Is it?" She hadn't noticed. Not with him around.

The pads of his fingers pressed into her skin. He brought his other hand up and covered it, rubbing her entire hand between both of his large ones in an effort to give it warmth. "I am assuming your gloves were stolen along with everything else. I have gloves in my satchel. Do you want them?"

The strength and heat of those long fingers penetrated her to the bone. She could only imagine what the man could do with those fingers in a bed. She needed to go to church. "No, thank you." She quickly descended the narrow, iron steps and landed onto the gravel path, away from a large patch of mud. She tugged her hand loose, trying to focus.

He turned and climbed up onto the back of the coach, retrieving a large wool satchel. Draping it onto his broad shoulder, he jumped down, strode toward her and grabbed her hand back as if it were his to grab.

Startled, she tried to tug her hand loose but his fingers were too strong. "What are you—"

"It will keep your hand warm and ensure every man knows you cannot be accosted." He smiled down at her, wove his heated fingers effortlessly between hers and clasped them snugly against his own.

A part of her soul liquefied. Her husband had never held her hand for the sake of warming it or for the sake of anything else. They'd never had that sort of relationship.

She glanced up at Mr. Levin, scrambling to keep up with his long-legged stride, while still holding his hand. Girlish though it was, she liked the attention. It was…sweet.

He kept walking, his thumb now skimming her palm.

Her eyes widened. Why was she, a titled lady of forty, permitting this? "We really shouldn't be holding hands," she said rather stupidly. "It isn't proper."

He eyed her. "I agree." He released her and shoved his hands into his coat pockets. Still striding alongside her toward a shadowed, stone building lit by lanterns that lined the wide road, he gruffly said, "You have very soft hands. Do you know that?"

She bit her lip hard. This had trouble slapped all over it.

LESSON THREE

Sometimes a man must refrain from being a man.

-The School of Gallantry

Once the room had been paid for and a brass key was in his pocket, Konstantin strode across the dirt pounded floor of the dilapidated lobby toward Lady Stone. She lingered by the narrow staircase leading to their lodging, scanning the brusque men around them. Men who boisterously spoke in Russian to each other in between splashing gulps of ale and vodka in tankards they staggered around with.

She seemed surprised. Little did she know, Russians were known to stay up all night and drink, whether they were travelling or not.

Konstantin continued to watch her. It was the first time he'd seen her in full light. She was stunning. Her travelling gown was sumptuous with all that expensive velvet and was hooked up to her chin in a refined elegance that made him want to whistle. She was curvaceous and tall. Being a touch over six feet himself, he'd never met a woman who reached his own nose. Yet she did. Her thick, dark brown hair was primly pinned up into a chignon that had grown lopsided from hours of sleep.

It didn't make her any less attractive.

From the moment she and that expensive perfume of hers had nestled into his lap hours earlier, he had a strange, glimmering feeling they were going to imprint their breaths on each other. He couldn't explain it, but he felt very protective of her. Like she was already his.

It was why he'd taken her hand.

And then there was the subject of the Glorious Midnight Bane. He wondered what meeting her at midnight could possibly mean. Konstantin tightened his jaw and refused to think about it. All he knew was that she needed a hero, and after too many years of being a criminal, he was more than ready to play the role of a hero to a beautiful woman who thought he was nothing more than a respectable man. It was nice.

He approached.

She turned, and adjusting the shawl around her cloak, skimmed his appearance from chest to boots without any attempt to conceal her interest in his physique.

His chest tightened, knowing that look all too well. The last time a woman gave him a look like that, he'd been left unconscious and bleeding on the floor. He had to avoid a repeat of that.

Konstantin strode up to the steep, wooden staircase and leaned against the unevenly nailed railing. "The innkeeper mentioned there was a sizable bathhouse in the courtyard. Would you like hot water prepared for you before you retire? It would be no extra cost to us."

Her pink, full lips pursed in due seriousness. "I'm exhausted. But tomorrow morning I will certainly take advantage of the offer."

"Consider it done. We ought to retire then. 'Tis late." He pushed away from the railing and swept an open hand toward the stairs. "After you."

"Thank you." She breezed past, filling the air once again with expensive perfume that reminded him of a cinnamon-tinged rose. It was a scent that suited her. Reserved but spicy. She gathered her dark green velvet travelling gown and stiffly made her way up the staircase, her cloak bundling around her arms.

Konstantin gripped the wood banister and followed her up. He tried not to assess her bum hidden beneath the layers of those heavy skirts but the full curve of those hips that were accentuated by a well-synched corset kept taunting him. It was difficult to believe she had a twenty-one-year-old son and three daughters. Her son was only nine years younger than him.

He was a very bad man.

Once on the landing, he focused on getting to the room. Reaching a narrow door with the number 12 crookedly painted with red on its wooden surface, he dug into his pocket for the key and adjusted the heavy sack on his shoulder. With the turn of his wrist, Konstantin kicked out a booted foot, thrusting the door out of their way.

He swept a gallant hand toward the open door. "After you."

She hesitated and then walked into the small room, her gown rustling past his booted feet.

He entered after her and pushed at the heavy, oak door shut. Dropping the sack from his shoulder, he kicked it off to the side and leaned heavily against the door. He paused. He could feel his watch shifting against the inside of his pocket. It was telling him something. What exactly, he was uncertain of.

She dragged her shawl up to her chin and turned toward the narrow bed.

Fitting two people on that bed for a night of sleep would require vast imagination. Which meant only one of them was getting the bed. So much for sleep. Or anything else. Not that she would entertain the idea of anything else. She was a lady.

Pushing away from the door in exasperation, he thumbed toward the wool sack. "I have clean clothing in my travelling bag. You can borrow one of my linen shirts to sleep in."

She smoothed her hands against the thick, velvet skirts of her travelling gown. "I will be fine sleeping in this. Thank you." She removed her cloak and shawl and surveyed the small room that was barely a few strides wide.

At least it had a small hearth.

He knew the woman was used to far better lodgings. She was an aristocrat. The scraped oak timbers that lined the walls and the low ceiling of the room was overly rustic for a woman dressed in velvet and cashmere. And the moment she crawled into that bed, her body would quickly realize the tick was stuffed with rough straw, not plush feathers.

Why couldn't he have had enough money to impress the woman with her own room? More importantly, why couldn't he have met the woman *after* his crowned glory of one hundred thousand? "I apologize that the lodgings are a bit rough," he finally said.

She draped her cloak and shawl onto the bed, her features softening. "There is no need to apologize, Mr. Levin. I am incredibly grateful to have a place to sleep. Thank you."

Those dark eyes were so stunning when she softened. They became warm-liquored and soulful and hinted at a much softer woman hidden beneath. One that enjoyed nestling against a man during cold winter nights. He liked women who nestled. "You have very pretty eyes."

She lowered her gaze with a half-smile. "Thank you."

He was beginning to ramble like a fourteen-year-old meeting a pretty girl. Shifting his jaw, he placed his right hand onto the rosewood handle of the dagger attached at his waist. "Are you hungry? I have some dried peaches and apples in my sack."

"No thank you." Her eyes darted to where his hand gripped the dagger. "Do you always carry a weapon?" she inquired.

"Yes." He paused, realizing he probably shouldn't have admitted that. It represented his old life and not the one he was embracing. Still, he did know women liked a man who knew how to handle a weapon. He casually removed his leather belt and tried not to vaunt. "As my father used to say, Russia has no saints."

He carried the belt and dagger over to the small, lopsided side table beside the bed and set it down with a clatter. The side table wobbled in protest. He inwardly winced, realizing just how awful the accommodations really were and stilled the table with a hand. He turned back toward her and drawled, "Let us hope the ceiling holds up, yes?"

A bubble of a laugh escaped her. "It isn't all that bad."

"No, I suppose not," he muttered, glancing around. "I have seen worse." He scuffed the bottom heel of his boot across the uneven floors. "It appears clean. And fortunately, there is no signs of roaches. Yet."

She froze, a look of horror tightening her pale face. She glanced at the floors and looked as if she might leap into his arms at the sight of anything with an antenna.

He probably shouldn't have said anything. Not that he would mind her leaping into his arms. "Roaches are annoying but harmless."

She hesitated and then politely offered, "I suppose once we close our eyes, it will be no different than closing one's eyes in a hotel in Paris."

He bit back a smile, liking how unpretentious she was. There was clearly more to her than a pretty face and a pretty gown. "I take it you have been to Paris?"

She shook her head. "Not yet. But I have a trip planned. Have you ever been?"

He shook his head. "My finances have never really allowed for it. But I do intend to travel there sometime next year. Around June." After he settled into his one hundred thousand.

She paused. "I plan on travelling to Paris next year in June, as well."

"Do you?"

"Yes."

It was like they were asking each other whether Paris was next.

He quickly removed his coat and tossed it to the wooden chair by the door. He also removed his waistcoat and tossed that as well. "We should sleep." Or something like that.

"Yes. We should." She turned and quickly sat on the edge of the bed. She reached down and after a few attempts of swatting toward her shoes, she let out a breath and sat up. "Could you please assist me in removing my boots, Mr. Levin? I would do it myself but I cannot bend at the waist."

This could get dangerous. He adjusted his linen shirt, reminding himself only her boots were coming off and rounded toward the bed. He knelt before her. "Allow me." He wagged a hand toward her.

She gingerly stuck out one booted foot.

He gently grabbed her ankle. Pushing up a section of her velvet skirt away from those feet, he loosened the fastening on each black leather half-boot. He made a valiant attempt not to notice anything other than her stockings were snow white and made out of silk. And that she had incredibly shapely calves. And that her ankles were slender enough for him to ring his entire hand around them.

His calloused fingers grazed the smooth softness of her stockings as he removed the first boot. The luxurious feel made his chest *and* his entire body tighten. And that was just the stockings. He removed her other boot and tightly smiled up at her, trying to assure her that he wasn't taking liberties. Even though he was.

She slid her hands across her skirts and also smiled. That smile was warm and far more inviting than he had expected.

Setting aside both boots, he quickly rose.

"Thank you for your assistance."

"It was a pleasure." Too much of one. He gestured toward the narrow bed. "I ask that you take the bed." He thumbed toward one of the two chairs behind him. "I will settle into a chair." He considered himself to be a gentleman, after all. Not in his head, mind you, but in practice.

She glanced toward the wooden chair, her arched brows coming together. "How will you sleep?"

"I appreciate the concern." He went over to the chair and sat, tilting himself into it until it creaked in protest. "But I will manage."

"Are you certain?"

"Quite."

Her dark eyes brightened. "Thank you. For everything."

"I am more than happy to oblige." He shifted against the hard seat and tried to get comfortable. "Sleep well."

She hesitated, then rose and bustled toward him. To his astonishment, she leaned down toward him, her perfume caressing the air between them and delivered a quick kiss onto his cheek before turning and bustling back to the bed. "Thank you."

He froze. The feel of those full, soft lips against his unshaven face made him realize sleep was the last thing he wanted. He really didn't need this. He didn't need to start thinking about her, kisses and— She was an aristocrat. It would be like him trying to get involved with the Emperor's daughter. It wouldn't end well. Though she claimed to have no husband, as beautiful as she was, she probably had a lover. A very territorial one. Hell, he knew he'd be territorial over her if she was his.

Tightening his jaw, he watched her unfold the linen.

She regally arranged herself onto the bed with a rustle of her gown, her full velvet skirts bundling up to her knees. A very impressive and very delectable display of slim, stockinged legs now appeared in full view with attractive black lace garters tied below each knee to hold the silk in place.

Mother of God. He wanted those legs fully wrapped around his waist.

With pursed full lips and a lowered gaze, she drew up the linen and primly covered herself with it, eliminating his view of those shapely legs. She busily patted the linens around herself, clearly unaware that he was watching her.

Her glance eventually cut over to him. She smiled pertly. "Goodnight, Mr. Levin," she offered, settling herself against the pillow.

With difficulty, he inclined his head. "Goodnight, Lady Stone."

But no, it wasn't going to be a goodnight. It was going to be a *long* night.

Cecilia's eyes fluttered open. A lone candle in the far corner of the rented room and the red burning coals in the small hearth dimly pushed back the late-night shadows. She turned against the linens, her travelling gown making it difficult for her to move. Pale moonlight beamed through the narrow, dirt smeared window.

She couldn't sleep.

Pushing herself up, she paused, realizing Mr. Levin was not in sight. The lone chair he'd been sitting in had been pushed back. His coat, waistcoat and pocket watch were draped over his wool sack in the shadows a few feet away from the door.

Cecilia slowly scooted out from beneath the linens, pushing the linen away from her gown so it wouldn't tangle. Her stockinged feet landed on the uneven wood floors. She glanced down and cringed knowing the floors were rough. Her silk stockings would never survive it.

She yanked up her gown and scrambled to remove her garters knowing he wasn't around to see it. Although she managed to untie both of her garters, her corset made it impossible for her to roll them down far enough to even try to yank them off her feet. Huffing out a breath, she tossed the garters onto the bed and made her way over to the wool sack draped with Mr. Levin's belongings. She picked up his pocket watch to check the time and paused, its weight surprising her as the chain unraveled and swayed against the side of her hand. Oddly, her fingers tingled. It was as if she were touching something incredibly special.

Noting something was etched on the back of the silver casing, she turned it up toward herself and squinted at the faded letters. It was written in English. "Eternally yours at midnight," she whispered.

What could it mean? Usually, a name or initials were engraved on the back of a watch. The silver was heavily tarnished, hinting that it was old. Clicking open the dented casing, she blinked at the uneven hands, realizing it was almost three in the morning. Shutting it, she gathered up his clothing from atop the sack and carried his coat and waistcoat over to the chair in an effort to tidy the room. She hated when things were unorganized.

Draping everything onto the back of the chair, she carefully set his watch onto the seat, centering it and then glanced around the empty room again. If it was three in the morning, where was he? She hurried over to the closed door. Seeing the key had been left in the lock, she pulled it out and opened the door.

He had forgotten to lock the door.

Peering out into the candlelit corridor, Cecilia hesitated, and stuck her head further out beyond the doorway. The creaking of the old inn was all she could hear. She froze.

A stocky, young blond male smoking a half-cut cigar leaned against the peeling wall beside an open door that was a door down from her own. His yellowing, linen shirt was open to the waist, revealing a fit chest, and his stained wool trousers were barely affixed to his hips as if he had just finished entertaining every last woman in town. He inclined his head toward her and lifted his cigar to full lips. Dragging in a long, indulgent puff, he regarded her and slowly released the smoke he'd drawn in through his nostrils and his mouth as if he were making love to it. He smiled and said something conversationally in Russian.

She blinked. "Uh...forgive me, sir, but I don't speak any Russian."

The young man's brows popped up. "Ah." Sticking his cigar into the side of his mouth, he scrambled to tidy his appearance by sweeping back his hair from his eyes. He removed his cigar, cleared his throat and edged closer, brokenly offering in a heavy Russian accent, "Woman is...English?"

His English was certainly better than her Russian. "Yes, sir. I'm English."

He dashed out his cigar against the frame of the door and shoved it into his trouser pocket. Opening the door to his room, he swept a hand toward it, his eyes brightening. He pointed at her and then cupped his hand and pretended to drink from it to indicate that he was inviting her into his room for a drink.

She cringed but sensed he was actually trying to be nice in the only way a twenty-year-old could. She shook her head. "No, thank you. I have to—"

He yanked out his cigar from his pocket and held it out, offering that instead.

A startled laugh escaped her. "No, thank you, sir. I don't smoke."

He tucked away the cigar and hurriedly pulled out a deck of cards from his other pocket. He held up the warped deck and gestured to her and them himself, asking if she wanted to play.

Another laugh escaped her. "Whilst I appreciate all the generous offers, I am actually looking for someone." She tried to slow her speech in the hopes that he would understand. "Did you happen to see a gentleman leave my room? Do you know where he went?"

He squinted at her, shoving the deck of cards back into his pocket. "Man?"

"Yes. A man." She tapped at her hair. "Dark hair. Did you see him?"

He held up his hand high over his head and then hit each arm as if to demonstrate Mr. Levin's tall, muscled frame. He gestured down the corridor. "Outside."

Thank goodness there was a sighting. "Bolshoe spasibo," she offered. Thank you was the only Russian word she did know.

He pointed at her, grinning. "Russian." He wagged the tip of his fingers, insisting she say more in his language.

Something told her he would keep her in the corridor all night if she let him. "I'm so sorry, but I really should find my travelling companion." She smiled, closed the door behind her and locked it with the key, clutching it. "I wish you a good-evening, sir."

He hesitated and then pointed to himself. "Markov."

The boy was adorable. "Thank you for the wonderful conversation, Mr. Markov."

He inclined his head twice, searching her face. Falling against the wall beside his door, he slowly held up a wistful hand.

Russian men certainly were nice. It made a woman want to get lost in Russia. She swept down the narrow corridor in the opposite direction. Her feet grew colder against the rough wood as she hurried down the staircase. She winced, feeling splinters digging into the soles of her feet and glanced behind herself, shoving the key from the room into the bosom of her gown to keep herself from dropping it.

Coming to the bottom of the main stairwell, she scanned the dilapidated hall of the inn whose iron sconces crookedly hung from the uneven walls. It was eerily quiet. The main hearth filled with coal which had earlier seen countless people gathered around, glowed on its own.

Clutching the folds of her skirt, she noticed a side entrance leading into the darkness that had been left open. She hurried out through that door. "Mr. Levin?"

The crisp, night air frilled the skin beneath her gown with gooseflesh. Her stockinged toes suddenly sunk into icy, thick mud. She groaned, jumped toward the stone path and darted into a barren side garden. Fortunately, it wasn't freezing outside and the snow was completely melted. "Mr. Levin?" she called out again. "Are you out here?"

He was nowhere to be found.

Oh, God. What if something happened to him?

The night was remarkably still as a large, full moon sat high, casting a vibrant white glow across the shadows. Unnerved breaths escaped her, frosting the air as she hurried into the garden past a small stable illuminated by the brightness of the moon. Earthy smells filled her nostrils as horses quietly neighed, some poking out their shadowed heads, acknowledging her presence.

She glanced around the isolated mossy grounds and large, shadowed trees and froze. A faint, golden glow from the planked crevices of a small wooden bathhouse greeted her.

She blinked. Was he…*bathing*? *At this hour*?

Cecilia gripped the fabric of her gown. Pinching her lips, she envisioned his broad back and wet, flexing muscles covered in soap and his black hair dripping and hanging into those green eyes. Given the bulk of his arms that had strained his travelling coat, she was quite certain there was plenty more attached to whatever she could envision. It was time to go.

Scuffing steps from behind made her snap toward the sound.

The shadow of a very large man resembling a gorilla emerged from the stables. He staggered and made his way toward her. Slurring something in Russian, he unbuttoned his trousers and shoved the flap of his trousers down. He yanked out a stubby cock.

Her eyes widened as the hairs on her nape stood on end. She darted straight for the door of the bathhouse. "*Mr. Levin*!" She prayed to God he was in that bathhouse. "*Mr. Leviiiiin*!"

LESSON FOUR

Have faith in your worth as a man and

a woman of worth will have faith in you.

-The School of Gallantry

Upon hearing his name in English through the haze of sleep he had unknowingly succumbed to after a *very* successful session of masturbation where he'd imagined Lady Stone doing all sorts of things to him, Konstantin sat up, sending a whirling splash of water around the massive wooden tub. He glanced toward the plank door of the bathhouse. The influence of the hot water and the lone candle waving inside the glass-encased lantern had lulled him into a sleep he hadn't been able to find earlier.

Had he imagined Lady Stone yelling for him? He'd certainly imagined her yelling beneath him in pleasure a moment ago. He surged to his feet, water streaming from his naked body. Climbing out of the massive tub, which took some effort given its size, he snatched the towel the innkeeper had provided him and got out.

The door to the bathhouse banged wide open as Lady Stone

skidded inside. "*Mr. Levin*! A man...he...*help*!"

His heart pounded in utter disbelief as he smacked the towel against his exposed cock. The colder evening air licked his wet skin as he stared wordlessly down at Lady Stone who was almost on top of him.

She frantically pointed toward a man outside of the bathhouse.

The man was urinating.

The oaf peered at them from over his shoulder and sniffed loudly, finishing his business with an unrefined tug of his trousers. Staggering away, he slurred something in Russian about horses defecating too much and disappeared back into the shadows of the stables.

Konstantin eyed Lady Stone. "You are safe."

Her full breasts rose and fell. "I...I'm so sorry." She edged back and back, her stockings visibly muddy. She stared at the towel he had barely bundled against his lower half and tried to grab the door to close it but kept missing because she was too occupied with looking.

He officially felt attractive.

She smacked her hands over her entire face. "I can't believe you're—" She jerked away and turned toward the narrow open door. She slipped against the wet boards. "*Ah*!"

He jumped toward her and grabbed her by the waist hard to keep her from falling and hitting her head against the nearest plank wall. He stumbled against the wetness of the wooden floorboards, realizing he had dropped the towel and though he tried to balance himself with his own weight, he couldn't.

They fell back.

Turning his body to better take the impact, he savagely held onto her to keep her from getting hurt as the wooden ledge slammed against the back of his legs, stinging his flesh.

He tipped backward with her into the water.

She screamed, trying to grab for something other than him as soap suds and water rose up around them from the large round tub like a massive wave crashing to shore. Liquid warmth drowned out both air and sound upon impact, dunking them both.

He couldn't breathe as water rushed up his nostrils and burned his throat. Konstantin scrambled to sit in the tub, sputtering out water as he came up for air and yanked Lady Stone up and out of the water along with him by her arms. He coughed, trying to get the water out of his throat.

"*Pffff!*" She blindly staggered on her knees in the water between his well-spread legs.

He sucked in a breath knowing his cock was fully visible through the soapy water and that she was between his legs.

Her hands pushed away pasted strands of long dark hair from her forehead as water cascaded from unpinned sections that flopped down onto her shoulders. Pins plunked into the water one by one by one. She stumbled and steadied her hands against his bare chest.

She stilled, her velvet gown billowing around them as it covered almost every inch of the water. Except for where he and his cock were.

Her glistening face was now barely inches from his own.

"Do not look down," he offered in a low, cautionary tone.

She intently held his gaze. "Duly noted."

For some reason, she wasn't scrambling to get out. She also wasn't removing her hands from his bare chest. In fact, he felt those slim fingers slowly tighten their hold.

Konstantin searched her face, trying to remain calm. Her long dark hair floated around their waists in the water along with her gown. She looked very different. She looked less prim and more provocative.

He lowered his eyes unwittingly to her wet, parted lips, feeling trails of warm water trickling down his face and chin from his own hair.

The rustling of water and their unsteady breaths were the only sounds.

Her lips parted as she searched his face.

It was like she was waiting for him to do something.

His cock hardened. He could feel his erection pointing rigidly toward her in the water, demanding that she be the one. And although, yes and yes, he wanted to grab her and fuck her until all the water left the tub, he knew that would be taking advantage of a woman who had just been drugged and robbed barely thirteen hours ago. Hardly a nice thing to do.

He leaned back, trying to regain control over his lower half. As casually as he could manage, he rasped, "Do you require assistance getting out?"

She searched his face. "Uh…no. Thank you. No, I…" She glanced away and fumbled to get out of the wooden tub. The weight of her gown pulled her back. She stumbled against him in the water.

Konstantin steadied her. "Close your eyes. I have to get out." He rose and pressed both hands to his erection, trying to cover it.

She glanced up at his nudity, her eyes jumping to his protruding erection.

He shot her an exasperated look. "I asked you to close your eyes."

She slapped her hands over her face.

And he thought women of status were respectable. Ha. Climbing out, he snatched the towel up again from the hook and used it to dry himself, wishing his erection would subside. It didn't.

He scrambled to gather his clothes, yanked on his linen shirt and donned his undergarments and dark wool trousers, before shoving his feet into his boots without stockings. Fully dressed, Konstantin approached the tub she still sat in and held out a hand. "Allow me to assist."

She pressed her hands against her eyes. "Are you dressed?" she primly asked.

"Does it matter?" he chided. "You have already seen everything."

She winced. "Forgive me for that." She opened her eyes somewhat sheepishly and seeing that he was, in fact, dressed, quickly reached up and grabbed his hand.

He grabbed her other hand and yanked her up in one swoop, his muscles straining against the weight of her wet gown which was dragging her in the opposite direction. "It would be much easier if you removed your gown."

"There is no need. I will manage."

"But the weight of the water is going to—"

"I will manage, Mr. Levin." Holding onto his hand, she stumbled out of the tub and onto the floorboards, spraying water everywhere.

He scrambled back, realizing sections of his clothes were now drenched and sticking to his skin. He huffed out a breath in exasperation and released her hand. "I will wait outside whilst you…*manage.*" Shoving open the door of the bathhouse, he stepped out into the pale light of the moon. Shaking his head, he lifted his linen shirt from against his skin and wrung out whatever he could.

She staggered out after him, dripping wet and groaned as she clutched her clinging skirts. She smacked her sides, the sound as wet as she looked. "My only gown is soaked. *Soaked.*"

"It will be fine."

"So says a man with a sack full of dry clothing. I have no other clothes!"

"We will set your gown before the hearth and let it dry."

"It will take a whole day to dry a gown like this," she muttered.

"Fortunately for you, we do not travel for another two." Konstantin turned toward her, still wringing out his own linen shirt and paused, skimming her from shoulder to feet. Her wet, velvet dress seductively clung to every luscious curve of that body. Glorious, full breasts beckoned as they pressed against the wet fabric of her bodice.

She looked half naked.

Damn. He rolled his tongue against the inside of his cheek before blurting, "Might I ask why you followed me? Knowing I was bathing?" He had to know the answer to this one.

"I didn't know you were bathing," she argued. "For heaven's sake, it's three o'clock in the morning! Who bathes at such an ungodly hour?"

"I do." He shrugged. "I could not sleep." Not with her in the room. Sadly, masturbation was a very necessary evil. It was how he had survived without a woman this past year. He had never been one for prostitutes and the women he *was* interested in either snubbed him or never gave him more than a night due to their fear of their family finding out they were involved with a 'criminal'. When it came to women, it was pathetically obvious he was going to need that one hundred thousand to lure in what he wanted.

"You didn't even lock the door," she grouched as she wrung out section after section of her skirt in between uneven steps. "Fortunately, we seem to be surrounded by decent people. I met a man next door to ours. He was incredibly pleasant."

"I am certain he was."

"What is that supposed to mean?" She kept walking unevenly against the weight of her gown, the fabric dragging and dragging against the stone path.

Following the glistening stream of water she'd trailed, Konstantin smirked and fell into stride beside her knowing she clearly needed help. "Turn toward me."

She jerked to a halt. "Why?"

"You are barely walking." He knelt before her, grabbed up heavy sections of her wet gown and started twisting water out of the velvet. He focused only on the task. Not that he was back to looking at her legs. He twisted and twisted and wrung the material around her gown harder until eventually half its weight was diminished.

She watched him from above and eventually said, "I find it difficult to place the sort of man you are."

He glanced up, releasing her gown. "Hm? What do you mean?"

"You appear to be a gentleman and are impressively well spoken in the English language and yet you don't even wear a cravat."

He'd been accused of that before. "I had a rather unusual upbringing. My father was a privileged gentleman who veered off the respectable path." He made sure *not* to mention how.

"Have you ever been married?" she prodded.

He rose to his feet, straightening. "No. Why do you ask?"

Those prim features wavered in the shadows of the garden. She shrugged and quickly looked away. "I was curious, is all."

By God. Was it possible she was actually interested in getting to know him? As a person? As a man? This was a first. And he didn't even have one hundred thousand in his pocket yet. "Uh…I was engaged once. When I was younger. She was from a fairly decent family but my father didn't approve. He was very protective of me. So he hired a few men to investigate her life and it was discovered she was seeing three other men. It hurt but I got over it. Since then, I was involved with a few women but it always ended with my face against a floor. I make poor choices when it comes to women. I want the moon but can only afford peat moss." He tapped at his head. "I am not very nimble."

Her eyes caught and held his. "I find that difficult to believe, Mr. Levin."

"So says the woman who is *not* involved with me. Hardly helpful."

A bubble of a laugh escaped her.

He smiled and leaned in. "Tell me more about yourself. You said you have a son and three daughters. Which, in truth, astounds me. What are their ages and names?"

She smiled as if he had finally introduced a topic she could gush about. "John is my eldest and the one I came into Russia for. My second eldest is Giselle. She is sixteen. Abigail is fifteen and then there is my youngest, Juliet." Her tone softened. "She is thirteen and is always at the cook's elbow. There isn't a thing that child won't eat."

He searched her face. Listening to her made him realize just how little he had seen of life as a man. He missed having a family. Here he was at thirty and what did he have to show for it? Nothing but all the fists he had dodged. "They sound endearing."

Her smile widened. "They most certainly are."

That smile said it all. She was part of a happy family. The sort a man rarely saw. "I take it you were happily married, as well?"

Her smile faded. She looked away. "Whilst I am close to my children, my husband and I were not so fortunate. Which was to be expected. He married me for my youth and I married him for his money."

He shifted away, his brows going up. "I am rather surprised. You appear to be a bit more passionate in nature than to settle for anything less than what beats in your heart."

She didn't look at him. "The heart does not pay bills, Mr. Levin. My mother married for love and it taught me well. Whilst my father was titled, he had very little to his name. We struggled to keep creditors from our doors all our lives and lived off the generosity of relatives who openly mocked us. One relative, in particular, wanted me to marry his son as if I owed him my hand in matrimony for all of the financial assistance my father had been given. I did not want that for myself and therefore settled on a relatively better man. Above all else, I wanted financial stability away from my relatives."

"Judging by your tone, you seem unhappy with the decision you had made."

She shrugged. "My husband was not unkind. He was a much better man than my cousin and he knew when to be generous."

"Yet he was not generous enough to make you happy."

She said nothing.

He quietly waited for her to say something else.

She didn't.

Which meant this conversation was at an end. He gestured toward the side door leading into the inn. "We should sleep."

She blinked rapidly, nodded and hurried past, the soft scent of her perfume clinging to the night air. She made her way into the inn, up the narrow stairs leading to their room.

Konstantin dragged in a ragged breath, inwardly savoring that beautiful scent and raked back his damp hair several times in an effort to remain calm. He strode up the narrow staircase after her until he reached the landing and the door leading to their room. He flicked a finger against the sleeve of her wet gown. "You cannot stay in this. It needs to dry."

She huffed out a breath. "I know." She pulled out the brass key from her bosom and paused, blinking down at the slightly open door. "I thought I had locked the door."

Shite. Konstantin pushed her back and away. "Go downstairs," he whispered. "Now."

Although she scrambled back, she whispered back, "I'm not leaving you alone."

"*Quiet.*" He creaked the door open and peered into the darkened room, noting the coals in the hearth barely glowed. Nothing moved. No one was in the room. Odd. He paused. "Are you certain you locked the door?"

"Yes." She held up the key and wagged it. "I locked it. I know I did."

He opened the door wider to better see into the room. Dim light slithered further in. Although no one was in the room, he sensed something wasn't right. "Stay where you are."

She froze.

He strode toward the oil lantern on the side table and stumbled against something at his feet. He kicked away a bundle of material from around his foot. Was that his sack? He headed toward the side table beside the bed and stumbled against something else on the floor. His shirt? He caught himself on the bed with a hand.

Grabbing the flint box, which he was now able to make out, Konstantin struck it and held it to the wick of the oil lantern on the side table. When the wick lighted, he shifted the glass back onto the brass holding and turned.

Strewn across the floor were his clothes, his undergarments and everything else that had once been neatly organized in his wool sack.

Everything lay scattered as if someone had been looking for something.

Someone had picked the lock.

He scrambled to the loose floorboard where he had hidden his money and plied it open. A breath escaped him seeing the small leather satchel with bank notes and coins. Releasing the floorboard and hitting it back into place, he paused, scanning the room.

Only one thing appeared to be missing: his watch.

It was not where he had left it with his coat.

His pulse roared as he swung toward her. "Someone picked the lock."

Her eyes widened as her hands gripped the wet fabric of her gown hard. "Did they take anything?"

"My watch." He grabbed his dagger off the bedside table and unsheathed it. Jogging toward the open doorway, he glanced left and right but saw nothing out of the ordinary. "You said you were talking to someone. A man."

"Yes, but—"

"Did you know what room he emerged from?"

She hurried in beside him and pointed to the door next to theirs. "There. But I don't think he—"

"Stay in the room. Regardless of what happens, bolt the door."

"Bolt the door? You don't mean to—"

"*Stay in the room.*" He stalked toward the door she had pointed to and using his boot, hit the door, rattling it several times against its hinges.

"*What are you doing?*" she hissed, leaning out of the doorway.

He glared. "He saw you leave the room. He was waiting for an opportunity."

She glared back. "Whilst I am not looking to defend a man who offers a woman a cigar and cards in the hopes of garnering her attention, you don't *know* if he picked the lock. It could have been anyone."

Oh, no. He knew the way these criminals conducted business. He'd grown up in it.

The door swung open.

A hefty young man with his yellowing linen shirt pulled over his trousers peered out at him. He froze, his blond, wavy hair falling into his eyes and said in harried Russian, "I took nothing."

Konstantin tightened his hold on the dagger. "Which means, you took something. Where is it?"

"*Mr. Levin,*" Lady Stone called out in exasperation. "Is it necessary to point that at him?"

"Yes, it is necessary," Konstantin called back in riled English. "Now stay in the room!"

The man edged out and glanced toward Lady Stone, his blond brows popping up. He glanced toward Konstantin. "I met her earlier. Is she your wife?"

"My wife?" Konstantin echoed. "No."

"Your sister?"

"No, she—"

"I love the British." The young man's tone purred. "They are my people. Tell her my cousin went to Truro for work in Cornwall. Everyone there was very generous. It changed his life. Has she ever been to Truro? Does she speak any Russian? What is her name? Tell her I work as a mason and am available. Tell her I am willing to learn English."

Konstantin lowered his blade in disbelief. Why was he suddenly jealous? "I came to your door, not to make formal introductions but to inform you we were robbed."

The man winced and scrubbed his head. "Ach. Yes. That. I will admit, sir, I…I went into her room looking for…for a stocking of hers. I collect them. But I took nothing else." He gestured toward the disheveled area behind the door. "Search my room."

Jesus. The man was a bloody deviant. "You went into our room looking for her stockings?"

The man hesitated, as if realizing his stupidity. "The door was open."

Konstantin grabbed the man by the shirt and slammed him into the nearest wall, causing the sconces around them to jump. "Unfortunately for you, my stupid friend, my watch is now missing. So tell me. Where the hell is it? Where did it go?"

"I…I do not know," the man choked out. "I did not take it. I only took a garter!"

"*A garter*? You bloody took her—" Konstantin pressed the tip of the knife into that throat and through gritted teeth bit out, "I want the garter *and* the watch. Or you are dead. And I will warn you, I fucking mean it."

The man's eyes widened.

"*Mr. Levin!*" Lady Stone bustled toward him. "Let him go! 'Tis obvious by the way he is panicking he didn't take it."

Seeing his blade pricking into the skin of a breathing person, and in front of a woman, no less, Konstantin's hand trembled. This was who he used to be. Not what he wanted to be. Damn it.

Konstantin released the man with a shove and stepped back, trying to remain calm. "You have until morning to give both back," he growled out in Russian. "Or I will find you. And God help you *and* your cousin from Truro when I do."

The man stumbled back into the room and slammed the door,

bolting it from inside.

Konstantin hissed out a breath. Never mind the garter, how in hell was he going to get his watch back? He veered toward Lady Stone. "He picked the lock to steal one of your garters."

Her chest rose and fell in visible breaths. "What? Why?"

"Apparently, he took a fancy to you. Next time, I suggest you not initiate men you do not know."

Her eyes sharpened. "Should I include you in that list of men? Because your behavior was uncalled for. The man was defenseless and had no means of protecting himself against your blade. He wasn't even trying to fight you!"

His lips parted. A man breaks into *their* room for *her* garter, takes *his* watch and somehow *he* was the villain. He shook his head, stalked past her and back into the room. She wouldn't be the first woman to treat him like this. He was always the villain. Never the hero. Always the villain.

Depositing the blade back onto the small rickety table beside the bed with a clatter, he kicked his belongings bit by bit into one pile and as calmly as he knew how, said, "Setting aside your garter, that watch is all I have left of my father. And now I may never get it back."

She lingered in the open doorway as if ready to leave. "What I just saw was a very different man from the one helping me." She stared. "Who are you really, Mr. Levin? Why do you carry a blade?"

He said nothing.

"You had best tell me."

"It is best you do not know."

"*Tell me.*" Her voice quaked. "Before I walk to Saint Petersburg on my own. Don't think I won't. After what I just witnessed, I deserve an explanation."

He momentarily closed his eyes, knowing he had no choice but to explain. Before she *did* walk to Saint Petersburg. Damn it. Damn it, damn it, damn it. It was every woman all over again. He re-opened his eyes. "Like my father before me, I used to protect influential criminals from being killed by the government. I have been doing it since I was eighteen."

Her lips parted.

"It paid well," he argued. "And the community of men involved were dependable and decent. We were like brothers. It only ever got rough when we were on assignment and had to travel with whoever we were commissioned to protect. But I am no longer doing it. I grew tired of people always thinking the worst of me. Especially women. Do you think good, respectable women want to marry into a life where the husband gets shot at? Far from it." He adjusted his shirt. "Which is why I am going to London. I am being given a chance to be what I should have always been: a better man. I am trying to be a better man."

"You call putting a knife to a man's throat *trying*?" she echoed.

He swiped his face. "I have never killed anyone. I have bruised and bloodied people beyond recognition, as my job required, but I have never killed anyone."

Her expression stilled. "Why didn't you tell me any of this earlier?"

He sighed. "Because if I had told you, you would have never allowed me to help you. And you needed help. I needed you to trust me. Given who I am, women never do. 'Tis always a dilemma."

She remained quiet.

God only knows what she thought of him now. "I am not going to hurt you. It is not who I am. Now please. Close the door and allow us both to get some sleep. It is late. You can yell at me in the morning."

She puffed out a breath. "I am not going to yell at you." Closing the door, she locked it with the turn of the key and wandered over to the chair where his coat and waistcoat were. "In truth, I feel partly to blame. I was looking at your watch earlier and left it out on the chair." She paused. Quickly leaning behind the chair, she lowered herself to the floor and swept something up with a clatter. Rising again, she turned toward him and held up his watch by its silver chain. "It must have fallen."

He swallowed in disbelief and collapsed onto the bed beside him, pasting his hands against his face. Not only had he threatened an idiot at knifepoint, he had also confessed to being a criminal and now *he* looked stupid.

He heard her bare feet pad over to him.

Keeping his hands against his face, he refused to look at her.

A soft breath escaped her. "We all do things we regret, Mr. Levin. And it is fairly obvious you wish to move away from your past. I cannot and will not hold that against you." Her tone was genuine and yielding.

It was not a tone he expected from her after what she had just witnessed and what he had shared.

Konstantin lowered his hands and glanced up at her.

Her long wet hair clung in lopsided sections to the sides of her concerned face.

It was like meeting who she truly was.

His throat tightened. "I vow unto you that I have never killed anyone. It is not who I am."

She leaned in and whispered, "I believe you. And your confession is enough for me to understand the sort of man you really are. Most men try to paint themselves as being more. Not less." Taking his hand, she gently clasped the cool metal of the watch against the palm of his hand.

"Know that despite your past, you have a friend in me after everything you have done *for me*. You didn't have to help me but you did. It says a lot about you."

The chain slipped through his fingers and dangled, swaying from side to side. He hadn't had a woman poke at his soul in a long, long time. It felt good. She made him feel good. Something he could hardly even do on his own. "Thank you," he murmured.

She nodded and wrapped her arms tightly around herself. She stepped back, trembling and glanced toward the low-burning hearth. "Are there more coals?"

Realizing the damp clothing had probably chilled her beyond what he should have allowed, he set aside the watch and scrambled to his feet. "I will add more coals at once, but we need to get you out of those clothes first."

She trembled.

"Turn around." He spun her around and unhooked the wet, heavy fabric down the curve of her back.

She stilled.

"I promise not to look at anything I should not." He unhooked the last of her gown down toward her back and tried to even his breathing realizing he was undressing her. He dragged her gown off her cool shoulders and arms, exposing an expensive looking satin corset, a sheer wet chemise and pale skin.

It took every ounce of respect he had for her to keep himself from gaping. He tugged the sleeves off her arms completely and yanked the gown down the length of her body, letting it drop to the floor in a heavy, wet heap. Determined to stay focused, he unlaced her corset and tossed it onto the floor as well.

Quickly turning away, so he wasn't imposing on her state of undress, he pulled the linen off the bed. Wrapping her tightly in it, he rubbed its warmth into her and smoothed away her wet hair from the sides of her face. "Remove your chemise."

She turned away, slipping out of it beneath the linen he had wrapped around her.

Konstantin gathered her clothing and corset and dragged the chair over to the hearth. Adding more coals into the hearth from the dented tin bucket, he laid her clothing out as close to the heat of the glowing coals as safety would allow. "Put your chemise and stockings here by the fire, as well. It should all be dry before we leave for Saint Petersburg the day after tomorrow."

She plodded over and dragging another chair over to the fire, draped her chemise and stockings against it. She softened her voice. "Thank you."

He nodded and strode toward his clothing he had yet to gather off the floor. He leaned over, picked up one of his linen shirts and tossed it toward her. "That can be your nightdress."

She caught the shirt with one hand and fumbled to pull it on without losing the linen.

Konstantin swung away to give her privacy. He grabbed his pocket watch off the bed, walked over and tucked it into his waistcoat pocket which was slung over the chair. Pacing back and crouching, he started gathering his belongings and shoving them into his wool sack, realizing his hands were trembling. He continued shoving the rest of his clothes into the sack knowing he was already smitten by a woman bold enough to confess that a man who used to protect criminals was worthy of even having a friend.

God save his stupid soul. Why did she have to be an aristocrat? Nothing would ever come of it.

LESSON FIVE

Do you remember what it is like to feel your heart beat again?

-The School of Gallantry

Cecilia hesitantly touched the side of her head, her cold fingers grazing long, wet hair which had cascaded from its pins in spiraling, unraveled sections around her shoulders. She gathered her hair, bundled it up, and tightly pinned each section into place using whatever pins she could find lodged in her locks. When everything was properly secured again into the chignon, she let out a breath.

What a night.

She patted her wet clothes into place against the back of the chair one last time, knowing she was wearing nothing but a linen shirt in the presence of a man she had just met. Why did she feel like a virgin all over again?

Smoothing the front of Mr. Levin's shirt with a hand that was hidden deep within the sleeve, she glanced down, making certain not too much of her legs were showing. The shirt smelled like him. Like charred wood. Rolling the sleeves several times, she finally caught sight of her hands.

"Are you dressed?"

She jumped at the sound of his deep, accented voice. She crossed her arms over her chest knowing her breasts and the outline of her entire body was very visible through the material. "Barely, but yes."

He turned and paused, his eyes trailing the length of her. He snapped his gaze away. Toward the hearth. "We should sleep."

Her heart fluttered, sensing sleep was the last thing he wanted. She eyed him.

His wet, black hair was casually raked back, accentuating those husky features and bright green eyes in a way that made her want to keep looking at him. His linen shirt was wide open to his abdomen, showcasing a muscle-defined chest and a well-chiseled stomach.

Gad was he ever beautiful. And that didn't include what she had seen in the bathhouse.

He thumbed toward the chair, still not looking at her. "I will take the chair."

She doubted he would get any sleep that way.

He settled into the chair and slid down, resting his neck on the curve of the wood. He stretched out long, trouser-clad legs, keeping his eyes on his boots. "Good night, Lady Stone."

She crossed her arms tighter against her breasts. She couldn't let him sleep in that chair whilst she took the bed. It wasn't a large bed, she knew, but it also wasn't the smallest, either. They could fit. "Would you rather sleep with me, Mr. Levin?"

"No."

"You would sleep better," she softly pressed.

"I doubt it. You are half naked and I can see everything through the linen of that shirt."

Her cheeks warmed knowing he actually looked.

He closed his eyes and crossed his arms over his chest, shifting against the chair. "I ask that you get into bed, Lady Stone. I am trying to do the right thing."

She couldn't believe this man had ever been involved in criminal endeavors. He was far too honest. And too nice. "Mr. Levin."

His eyes remain closed. "What?"

"You paid for the room. You deserve good rest."

"If you cease talking, *dorogaya moya*, I will get rest," he gruffly said, eyes still closed.

"I am not about to desist."

His eyes snapped open. "You want me to sleep with you in that excuse of a bed? Knowing that our bodies will be touching?"

She pressed her tongue hard against the inside of her teeth. "We will manage." To demonstrate that she meant it, she crawled onto the bed and yanked the linens she carried over with her onto it. She could feel his eyes probing her as she pushed her bare legs beneath the cool linens and coverlet. Yanking his linen shirt down as far as it would go, lest it show off more than it already did, she scooted as far over to the edge as possible. And waited.

He sat up in the chair and said something in Russian.

"Pardon?" she asked.

He fell back against the chair, setting both hands against the sides of his head. "I am a former criminal who has not lain with a woman in almost a year."

"You could have taken advantage of me many times. But you didn't. Did you?"

His hands dropped.

She yanked the linens up to her chin and sank against the pillow. "Are you coming?"

He huffed out a breath. His chair creaked as he rose from it.

As conversationally as she could, she offered, "With our backs to each other, we will fit."

The floorboards creaked beneath his weight as he made his way toward her. He paused beside the bed and lingered. "Lady Stone."

She tugged the linen down from her chin and glanced up at him. "Yes?"

Dragging a hand through his still-damp hair, he dropped a heavy hand back to his side. "Why do you continue to trust me?"

It was endearing that he actually sought to protect her from himself. "You have more than proven yourself, Mr. Levin."

"Have I?" His voice came low. "I should probably tell you I wanted to take advantage of you back in the bathhouse. And even worse, I am *still* thinking about it."

She captured his intent gaze, a dizzying current overtaking her. Flashes of their naked bodies pressing and gripping and grinding caused her heart to skid. "I can assure you," she warned half-seriously, "you are not the only one thinking about it. So don't consider yourself to be a rebel."

His green eyes darkened. "Knowing that neither of us can be trusted, you are *still* going to insist I get into bed with you?" he asked, spacing his words evenly.

A pulsing knot rose within her throat. Being ravaged by him wouldn't be the worst thing to have happened to her in seven years. "I trust you."

He pushed out an uneven breath as if buying time. "Did you latch the door?"

He knew she did. She tightened her hold on the linen. "Yes."

He removed each boot from his feet, letting each thud heavily as it landed on the floor. "Do you mind if I undress before I get into bed?"

Her heart felt as if it were going to burst into pieces. "No."

He peeled off his linen shirt, all of his smooth, well-defined muscles rippling from the movement. His dark, damp hair fell into his eyes as he bundled the shirt. He tossed it, causing the bulk in his arms to flex, emphasizing a fresh, angry scar on his bare left shoulder and now stood only in trousers slung overly low on narrow hips.

Her knees locked together and the room almost swayed. It was the bathhouse all over again. Not that she was complaining. Trying desperately to focus, she asked, "What happened to your shoulder?"

He glanced at it. "I was shot a few months ago for protecting a man who did not deserve to die. It is what made me walk away from the life I was leading. It made me realize I was promoting the violence."

There was something remarkable about a man willing to get shot for another man. She held his gaze. "Does it still hurt?"

His rugged features softened. "No." Edging in, he bent down near her, his bare chest and the bulk of his arms obstructing all view. He leaned in close. And then closer, still. So close, the heated scent of his soaped skin penetrated the air between them. "If you were not a lady, would I have a chance?"

She inhaled sharply at the unexpected question. Something told her he was about to kiss away everything she had ever known. "Do you really want me to answer that?"

"No. It is best you do not answer." He straightened, leaned over to the side table beside the bed and extended his muscled arm toward the lamp. There was a click of metal from the oil lamp wick being turned down to extinguish the flame.

Darkness blanketed the room.

"You are very brave for allowing this," he rumbled out.

A bubble of a laugh escaped her. "You haven't gotten into bed yet."

"Allow me to change that." The straw tick shifted.

She scooted over, gripping the edge of the tick so she wouldn't fall off.

He stretched out beside her and moved closer, causing her body to tilt toward him.

Her nails dug deeper into the tick beneath her.

He shifted closer and using a large hand, took hold of her hip in the darkness and yanked her backside against him, pressing her body against his own.

Cecilia's eyes widened, drowning in the heat of his soap-scented body. His front was against her backside.

He was quiet for a moment, then stated what they already knew. "This bed was not made for two."

That was an understatement.

He dragged up the linens against their bodies a bit more, tucking it against the curves of her body. "Are you warmer?"

Why did he have to be so divine? "Yes."

"Good." He shifted against her, his hand gently grazing her hair in the darkness. "You are a very stubborn woman."

Her entire body pulsed. "I am told it is one of my best qualities."

"Something tells me you have far better qualities." His hand drifted down from her hair. He smoothed the curve of her hip with an open palm, his fingers dragging against the linen that separated his hand from her skin.

Her heart thudded and melted all at once. In that moment she knew that if he initiated anything, she would kneel.

He kept smoothing the curve of her hip, the tips of his fingers slowly digging into her and the linen more and more.

She wanted to faint from want.

His hand left her hip and skimmed down her arm. "Do you have a lover back in London?"

This conversation had officially turned wild. "No. I have never taken a lover."

He hesitated, then leaned in and brushed her hair away from her neck. "Something tells me you are about to."

Those husky words and those fingers made her entire world sway.

His hand drifted down toward her breast. He slipped his hand beneath the linen, his calloused fingers grazing and roughing her hardening nipple. "Are you going to stop me?" His voice was ragged. Uneven.

She gripped the edge of the tick harder. "No," she choked out. There was no denying she wanted this. She wanted him.

He pressed his trouser clad hips into her backside hard, his stiff cock now digging into the lower curve of her back. He slowly ground into her.

She couldn't breathe. The heat of his erection penetrated the linen of the shirt she was wearing. She could feel wetness in between her own thighs and prayed he would just do it.

His fingers dug into her waist as the heat of his mouth lingered closer against her ear. "Remove everything," he rasped. "And if you say no to me, I am getting out of this damn bed and sleeping in that chair for two days."

She was too overwhelmed by her own desire to think anymore. She sat up, scrambled to yank off the linen shirt from her body to ensure there was no going back and whipped it aside. Turning toward him, she blindly grabbed his unshaven face, prickling her fingers and pressed her nakedness against his warmth.

His chest unevenly rose and fell against hers in the darkness. His hot, wet tongue traced her lips. "Admit it. You wanted me all along."

Her eyes closed in disbelief and slipped into his world. "I did. God, yes, I did."

"I knew it." His tongue parted her lips as his entire mouth grazed hers slowly and masterfully, before moving more urgently against hers. He angled his mouth against hers and pressed down harder until her lips stung and were forced to open wider against the demand of that rolling tongue that probed even deeper into her mouth.

Her fingers dug into him and his fingers dug into her as they feverishly kissed.

The savage need to climax was mutual. It pulsed from their skin.

She frantically smoothed her hands against his velvet, hard-muscled heat.

He shifted on top of her, pushing her down onto the narrow mattress. The quick movement of his fingers between them announced he had released the last button on his trousers. He captured her mouth again, tonguing her heatedly and positioned himself above her, shoving her legs wide open. He guided his cock toward her opening, the muscles in his arms and in his broad back tense against her roaming hands.

His length penetrated her in a single, violent thrust that slammed her into the mattress.

She gasped in complete disbelief of what she was doing.

Holding his rigid heat deep inside her, he released her mouth. "Do you need me to refrain and go slow? Or can I...get to it?"

She knew the answer to that one. "Get to it."

He kissed her lips for a lingering moment, slowly trailing his mouth down to her chin, then knelt and yanked her legs up onto his broad shoulders.

Her heart skipped.

Dragging both hands tightly up her legs, he heatedly pounded into her, relentlessly banging them and the bed harder and harder into the wall.

It wasn't the sort of sex she had *ever* had with her husband.

Each hard thrust caused her body to tense and ache in a way she desperately needed. Each hard thrust caused the bed to shift.

He growled something in Russian, penetrating her again and again with raw intensity.

Her heartbeat throbbed in her ears as her core tightened against each rhythmic thrust. She welcomed every moment of it between uneven, ragged breaths.

He slowed and lowered her legs back down onto the mattress.

She wrapped her arms around him, waiting for more. Wanting more.

His fingers dug into her wet hair. "I cannot believe you are allowing this." He jerked his thick cock in and out of her.

She frantically fingered the expanse of his muscled back in between uneven breaths she could barely manage and dragged her hands all the way down toward his waist. She wanted to touch and feel all of what she had seen in the bathhouse. Hard. Sculpted. Tense. And it was hers. All hers. To touch. To feel.

His smooth, heated skin now felt moist against her fingertips as he worked their bodies into a more frenzied state.

He said something in Russian.

She didn't need to understand to know he wanted more.

She pushed up into him, now desperately wanting to bring herself closer to what she had wanted all along: release. Release from her entire life. In that moment, she wasn't Lady Stone anymore. She wasn't what society expected her to be. She was Cecilia. A woman who had always secretly and ardently yearned to touch *real* passion. The sort of passion a titled lady could never give into without destroying her name.

She feverishly ran her hands up and down the length of Konstantin's firm, muscled back, and grabbed for his buttocks, squeezing them.

A muffled groan escaped both their mouths.

He stilled. In between ragged breaths, he rasped, "What is your birth name? You never told me."

"Cecilia," she barely managed.

He rolled his hips, forcing his cock deeper. "Cecilia," he breathed in between steady strokes. "By allowing this, you are damning me to needing you. You do realize that, yes?"

His hand slid down between them, making her gasp. He fingered her in between thrusts, his hand never stopping as he rubbed and rubbed her nub faster.

Her throat tightened as her body reached a heart-pounding peak that unexpectedly handed itself over to climax.

It came too soon.

She cried out and her body trembled in an explosive release that penetrated more than her body. It penetrated her soul.

His moist, hot mouth descended onto hers again, muffling her cry as his hand jumped out from between them. Gripping her waist tightly, he pulled her against himself one last time, until he gasped against her mouth and tensed. He pulled out of her wetness and seething out a savage breath against the curve of her throat which he had buried himself into, she could feel him jerking and jerking his hand faster against his cock in the darkness.

He groaned into her. She felt that groan penetrate every inch of her as his seed spilled all over her inner thighs. He groaned again and she could feel him spilling more. He seethed out another breath and smeared the wet warmth of his seed against her skin with the length of his cock.

He collapsed against her and buried his head once again into the curve of her throat. Wrapping his arms around her, he pressed her tightly against himself as if he didn't intend to ever let go. "You are so beautiful."

She tightened her own hold on him. How was it a complete stranger had shown her more passion and more desire than her own husband had in the fourteen years she had been married?

Konstantin lifted his head. "Cecilia," he whispered hoarsely, his chest heaving.

"Yes?" she whispered back.

A breath escaped him. He kissed her forehead softly and brought her closer, tucking her against that solid chest. "Words elude me."

She clung to him, the intake of his breath and her own pulse drumming in unison beneath her fingers. "They elude me, too."

He rolled her with him, so that he lay on his back and settled against the pillow, adjusting them so they could better fit on the narrow bed. "Are you comfortable?" he murmured into her hair.

"Yes, Mr. Levin, I am," she murmured back.

He gently tapped her bare skin. "No more Mr. Levin. You and I are lovers. That means you are Cecilia and I am Konstantin. Do you understand?"

None of this was real. How could it be? They had just met. "Yes. I understand."

Whatever was happening between them, whatever she had allowed for, didn't feel wrong. It felt beautiful. *He* felt beautiful. She nestled her cheek against his chest, refusing to think about anything but him. This was *her* time. Her girls were nowhere in sight and the *ton* were far, far away in another country well across an ocean and could not judge her. This was between her and what she wanted as a woman.

This was better than Paris.

LESSON SIX

Some wake up to find that their dreams have at long last come true.

Only…that is when the real nightmare begins.

-The School of Gallantry

Late morning

Konstantin opened his eyes and paused. The back of Cecilia's tousled, dark head was tucked below his chin and her smooth, naked warmth was spread across the length of his own nakedness. What had happened between them was real.

His throat tightened. Lifting his head, he glanced down at her. She continued to sleep, her breath coming in soft, even takes. Her full lips were parted and her pale face looked so beautiful and at peace. The linens were pulled around their entangled bodies.

It was the first time he'd ever slept in the arms of a woman for a full night. She felt like home.

He slowly dragged the linens away from her body and gently folded it down over her hip so he could look at her in a way he hadn't been able to at night.

Full, white breasts greeted him. Visible marks puckered her pale stomach from the stretching of each child she had carried. It didn't make her any less beautiful. It made her everything she was. He slid his hand down toward that stomach, reveling in her warmth and softness.

Tightening his jaw, he slid his fingers down to the short, curling black hairs between her thighs.

She startled and grabbed his hand hard, her chest rising and falling. "You scared me."

"Forgive me." He leaned toward her lips and kissed them, shoving aside the linens. "Did you sleep well, *dorogaya moya?*" He forced his hand in between her thighs. He pushed his finger deep into her, his cock hardening and using her wetness, slowly flicked his finger upward toward that nub. "I want you again."

Her lips parted as she watched his hand in between escalating breaths. She grabbed his thigh hard and held him in place against her backside.

He flicked her faster and ground his erection into her again and again until she was gasping. He withdrew his finger from her wetness and sat up, leaning against the headboard behind them. Dragging her up and onto his lap, so she faced him, he sat her up. "If only every morning were as bright as this one," he murmured up at her. "How are you, beautiful?"

She shyly smiled. "I am still in disbelief."

"You are not the only one." He slowly wrapped her legs around his naked waist and cupped her face with both hands, letting her dark brown hair cascade down over her bare shoulders and onto her breasts.

He held her gaze, wanting to believe that the reason they were doing this was because they not only wanted each other but needed each other.

She wordlessly lowered herself onto his cock and slid down onto his length.

He bit back a shudder and tightened his hold on her beautiful face, letting her take over. He traced the tip of his tongue across the curve of her chin, dragging it to her lips.

She slipped her hands onto his shoulders and slowly rode him.

He rolled up and into her, digging his fingers into her thick hair. He let his one hand trail down to her breasts and held up one. Lowering his head, he flicked his tongue over its slope and in toward the nipple until it hardened.

She threw back her head, arching toward him and rode him steadily faster. Tightening her long legs around him, she ground down again and again and again, making it harder for him to breathe through the stirring, building sensations. Pleasure rippled through his core and his body and his cock, tensing all of his muscles.

Pushing away her hair, he grabbed the back of her neck and buried his head into the soft curve of her throat, determined to leave his mark on her body. He sucked on the skin of her throat hard, pulling the skin in past his teeth.

She gasped. Digging her nails into his shoulders, she rode him.

Holding her waist, he gritted his teeth and jerked her down harder, wanting to go as deep as her womb would allow.

She cried out and rocked against him, her body quaking.

He couldn't hold it, either. He spilled into her wetness. Konstantin choked and quickly pulled out. Still shuddering, he finished spilling his remaining seed all over her stomach, his cock pulsing and his core tightening beyond what he could bear.

He yelled out.

In between ragged breaths, Konstantin wrapped his arms around her. Burying himself in the softness of her skin, he confessed in complete exasperation, "I spilled some of my seed into you."

Her head popped up from his chest, her hair wildly crossing the side of her face. "How much is some?" she demanded.

A nervous laugh escaped him. "Not enough to make me panic. We should be fine."

She adjusted the linens over herself and eventually confessed, "This is so unlike anything I have ever done with my life. I am usually very…*sensible*. I pride myself for my being respectable. I *am* respectable."

He smiled and tilted his head so as to better see her face, trying to decipher if she was pleased with the statement or not. "Do you have any regrets?"

A soft breath escaped her. "In truth, I have less regrets about this than I did when I married my husband."

His brows went up. "Was I that good? Or was I that bad?"

A laugh escaped her. "I only knew my husband for a week before I married him by special license."

He let out a low, long whistle. "And I thought we waltzed past introductions quickly."

She winced. "I was young and didn't want to marry my cousin who was practically banging on my door. Everyone expected me to marry him. But I wanted a respectable man. One who could provide me and my parents with the financial lifestyle we never had separate from the Gunther family. Given my husband's popularity, when he asked me to marry him by special license shortly after we met, I panicked and gave in. I knew nothing about men." She huffed out a breath. "I still don't."

He smirked. "Why do I feel this conversation keeps returning to me?"

She shoved at him playfully.

He nudged her playfully back. "Are you hungry?"

"Beyond famished."

"Good. I will get dressed." He pointed at her. "I ask that you stay in bed. I doubt your clothes are dry anyway." He slid out of bed and paused, realizing he'd never shared a morning meal with a woman after a night of sex. Knowing it, he leaned down and quickly kissed her on the lips. For good measure. "I will be back."

He dressed and in between the final straightening of his appearance and the buttoning his waistcoat, he glanced toward her, sensing she was watching him.

Those dark sultry eyes met his. She gushed into a smile.

It was a smile he had waited his whole life to see. It was a smile that promised him anything he wanted despite who he was. "I blame you for this," he said, pointing at her. "You seduced me."

She quirked a brow. "I did no such thing."

"So says the lady who insisted I climb into her bed." He smirked and grabbing up his pocket watch, tossed it to her, letting it land on the bed beside her bare foot. "Keep it safe whilst I am gone. God forbid it fall behind another chair."

She laughed, sat up and dragged it toward herself.

"Should I try to get your garter back from our neighbor?" he added.

She rolled her eyes. "Let him keep it. Heaven knows where it has been."

"Lucky bastard. How is it he gets a garter and I do not? I want one."

She tsked. "Will you feed me already?"

His mouth quirked.

A half hour later, he returned to the room with a massive wooden bowl filled to the rim with stew and two wooden spoons shoved into it. He closed the door after himself and locked the door. Turning back to her, he announced, "They did not have much."

"You make it sound like a terrible thing," she chided. "As hungry as I am, I will eat anything."

He paused.

She lay on her stomach, leisurely naked, opening and closing the silver casing to his watch with slim fingers. She smiled, brushing away long, unbound hair from the side of her face and adjusted the linens over her waist.

It was like walking in on a woman he had been married to for years.

His chest tightened. This would never last. How could it? She was an aristocrat with four children and he was a reformed criminal. He shoved the thought aside, refusing to think about it.

He strode toward her and sat on the edge of the bed next to her, setting the bowl beside her. "Tell me what you think." He prayed the food was half-decent.

She sat up, dragging the linens to cover her breasts. Dipping the wooden spoon into the stew, she leaned over and daintily scooped it up toward herself. Her lips closed around a mouthful before sliding the spoon back out. A muffled groan escaped her as she half-closed her eyes. "'Tis divine," she murmured. She hastily scooped up another heaping spoon. And another. And another.

He was glad she approved. Because after counting out what he could afford, knowing that they were leaving to Saint Petersburg tomorrow, he could only afford another meal and two tankards of ale. If they were lucky.

Even though he was hungry beyond breath, Konstantin nudged the bowl closer to her. "When you are done, I will eat whatever is left."

She paused in between another mouthful, then swallowed and lowered the spoon quickly back into the stew, leaving it. "Forgive me." She slid the lone bowl back toward him, licking her lips. "You should eat."

She was such an angel to him. He smiled and slid the bowl back toward her. "No. I am fine. Finish as much as you can."

"After you have some."

He shifted against the bed they sat on, knowing full well it was the only bowl they would have until evening. "I am not hungry."

"Are we back to arguing about the chair?" She pursed her lips, took up the other spoon and scooping up a heap full of vegetables and meat, held it out to him. "Open your mouth."

Now he felt like he was two. Why did he have to like her? "I will eat *after* you finish half the bowl. Agreed?"

"No. Not agreed. Because by then it will be too cold for you to enjoy," she pertly returned, still holding out the spoon. "Now eat."

"You barely had a few bites."

"Whilst you had none." She held the spoon closer to his mouth. "Do it knowing I want this for you more than anything in the world. Knowing I want you big and strong so you can rescue me from more garter stealing thieves. *Pleeeeease?*"

He sighed. This woman was going to take over his entire life. He leaned in and pulled the offering into his mouth. The savory, thick saltiness of chewy meat, potatoes and peas made him melt and half-nod in appreciation. "That is good," he said in between chews.

She grinned, a dimple appearing on her left cheek and quickly re-immersed the spoon into the bowl, filling it again. She held it out, her dark eyes brightly searching his face. "More?"

He held her gaze, glimpsing what she might have been like at twenty. Bright-eyed, ambitious, kind and daring despite her station in life. She was going to make him kneel to her. She was going to make him kneel to her. Never mind the Midnight Bane, she was going to make it impossible for him to walk away from whatever was happening between them. He could feel it in his chest. It was something he'd never felt in the presence of a woman.

He slowly took the spoon from her hand and returned it to the bowl. He tugged her fingers loose from it. "Kiss me."

She paused.

He leaned in. Brushing aside her long hair from her bare shoulder, his fingers skimmed the softness of her skin. "What is happening between you and me?" he whispered. "Is this even real?"

Her lips parted. "It feels real," she whispered back. "I want it to be real."

He heatedly searched those dark eyes. "Good. So do I." He gently captured her lips, giving into the idea that this could be the beginning of something incredibly special.

Too special to even try to name.

Evening

They had only left the room twice throughout the day. Once to share another meal and a tankard of ale at one of the wooden tables downstairs and the other time to soak in the bathhouse together, where they washed each other's hair and lathered each other in soap in between ardent kisses and sex. The remainder of the day, they lounged in each other's arms and talked like friends of old, discussing their childhoods, and how life had not exactly turned out the way they had hoped. They laughed at all the words Cecilia couldn't pronounce in Russian as Konstantin playfully traced Russian words onto her bare legs. They also made love. Repeatedly.

Getting robbed was the best thing to have ever happened to her.

Cecilia nestled against Konstantin's nude warmth as she watched the last of the light fade from the lantern with the curling of smoke, leaving them in complete darkness. Tomorrow evening, when they arrived into Saint Petersburg and called upon the theatre for her son's address, everything she had shared with Konstantin would shimmer away into a dream. She would have to abandon being a woman and return to being what she really was: a titled lady and a mother.

Konstantin brushed a finger across her arm in the darkness. "After we find your son, I will not be able to stay in Saint Petersburg. I have to leave for London."

She swallowed against the tightness overtaking her throat. Even he knew their time together was at an end. Although a part of her ached knowing it, she had to cease pretending she was an ordinary woman. She wasn't. She had a duty to her title, the estate, to her daughters and to her son and all of their respectable names. What *she* wanted did not exist in the realm of the *ton*. It never had and it never would. She had known that since she was fifteen.

He smoothed her hair away from her throat. "I would like to see you again in London. As soon as you return from Russia. Is that possible?"

She paused, her heart pounding. "You want us to continue this?" she whispered against him in disbelief. How could they?

"Of course I do. I…" He paused. "Are you telling me you are no longer interested?"

She pressed her cheek harder against his chest, cherishing how genuinely distraught he sounded. Maybe this didn't have to end. Maybe they could quietly meet on the outskirts of London every week. No one needed to know. Men of the *ton* did it all the time. What made them special? She wanted him. She wanted this. He made her feel beautiful. He himself was beautiful. "We will find a way to be together. I promise."

A smile appeared in his voice. "Good."

In the darkness, between her own pulse and his, the words '*Eternally yours at midnight*' popped into her head. She sat up against him in the darkness. "I forgot to ask. Your watch mentions the hour of midnight on the casing. Is there a story behind it?"

He shifted her body better against his own. "The watch belonged to my father. It was given to him by a woman he was supposed to have married. Unfortunately, she died before that happened."

Her stomach dropped to her knees. "I'm so sorry to hear it."

"Her name was Miss Bane."

"She was English?"

"Yes. My father's family thought her beneath his status, given he was the son of a well-known merchant, but he always financially struggled. Miss Bane was a governess from London, visiting her brother in Russia when my father met her at a festival. She was older than my father by about ten years. Much like…" He stilled, his fingers suddenly digging into her skin.

She swallowed. He didn't have to finish. She knew exactly what he was thinking. She blinked up at him, making out the shadowed outline of his face. "Surely, it is a haunting coincidence."

He hesitated. "I do not believe in coincidence."

Curious, she set her chin on his chest and ventured to ask, "What do you believe in?"

"Destiny. And that real love can go beyond death." A breath escaped him. "My father eventually moved on, many, many years later, and married my mother, but even my mother often told me that the largest part of my father's soul always belonged to Miss Bane. My mother simply learned to live with it. Apparently, my mother lost every child during the first five years of their marriage until I was born. Unlike the others, I chose to arrive into the world during the annual festival of Maslenitsa at exactly four minutes to midnight. Eerily, it was the same festival and hour my father had met Miss Bane. It haunted him. Growing up, I could sense whenever he looked at me, he expected me to announce that Miss Bane sent me with a message."

He fingered her skin gently. "My father and I were very close. I idolized him. Despite his profession, he was a very good man. He taught me everything. From pulling out a chair for a lady to breaking a man's nose." He nodded. "He always claimed incredible things happened at midnight and that I was proof of it." His voice cracked. "Deny it as I may, you and I met at midnight when you opened your eyes to me for the first time." He slid his hand down her back. "'Tis fairly obvious what Miss Bane and destiny has in mind for us."

Her heart squeezed.

He tightened his hold on her. "As my father always used to say, even if you do not believe in destiny, you will in time. Because everything happens for a reason. Which means, we will not be able to escape whatever destiny has planned. Even if we want to."

She pressed herself harder against Konstantin, closing her eyes in an effort to memorize the sound of his heart and the feel of his skin against her own. In that moment, she wanted to believe destiny was real and that *nothing* would keep them apart. Even though she knew, once they were both in London, *everything* would.

The following morning

Life had become so bizarrely perfect. It made a man wonder if something was about to go wrong. Not that it would. He had destiny and midnight on his side.

He stretched himself fully awake and dragged Cecilia's warmth closer against his own body. He kissed the curve of her throat, noticing he had left amorous marks all over her skin. Half of which he didn't even remember making. It was a long night. "'Tis morning," he murmured against her skin, trying to rouse her. "We should peer in on the time. Our stagecoach leaves at noon today."

She stirred and suddenly tightened her hold on him, digging her chin into the crook of his arm as if unwilling to let go.

He nuzzled her throat again before slipping his arms out from around her. He sat up. "We should get dressed."

"No. Wait." She scrambled up and out of bed, her bare feet thudding against the floorboards. She turned toward him, completely naked and announced, "I need you to dance with me. Before we do anything else."

His brows rose as he perused her nudity. "I think I have corrupted you beyond measure."

She leaned over the bed and grabbed at his bare arm, shaking it. "I once read that the women in France dance in the arms of their lovers naked. I want to try it."

He never saw *this* coming. Not from her. Pushing himself off the bed, he landed before her naked and held out his arms. "If it were any other woman, I would have said no."

She grinned. "Thank goodness I'm not any other woman." She reached up and primly set one hand on his shoulder and took his hand into hers and pressed herself close.

He lowered his gaze to her face, trying to focus on her and not that they were naked. He curved his other hand around her waist and set it against the middle of her smooth back. Dragging in a breath, he whisked her to their right and felt his cock swing with it. He cringed. "Pardon my friend."

She giggled. "It's incredibly awkward dancing naked, isn't it?"

"Very. It loses its grace. Clothes keep everything in place."

"Why do you think the French do it?"

He smiled. "Maybe we should go to Paris and ask them."

They turned and stepped as if dancing to music.

Cecilia searched his face, tightening her hold on his hand and shoulder, her long dark hair swaying against their movements over her bare shoulders. "You make me want to dance naked, Konstantin. Do you know that?"

His lips parted as he continued to quietly dance with her around the room, their bare feet now being the only sound. It was a moment that he, as a man, would remember for the rest of his days.

This was not the same, panic-stricken woman he'd first met.

This was a woman who had discovered she had been in control all along.

"When you get back from Russia," he murmured down at her. "I will take you to the best restaurants in London to make up for the lack of meals I subjected you to. I would also love to attend an opera with you. Is that something your girls would be interested in doing with us?"

She glanced up at him, her features flickering with unreadable emotion. She brought them to a halt.

He paused. "What is it?"

She lowered her gaze, her fingers trailing down his arms, toward his chest. "The rules in London are different for a woman of my standing. I...I have a responsibility to my name. There are, however, quiet inns on the outskirts of London where we could meet on a weekly basis." She paused. "It would be the only way I could see you."

He inhaled and exhaled. That hurt. More than he expected it to. He released her and rigidly stepped back. Why had he stupidly believed a woman willing to argue with him about whether he slept in a chair or whether he ate enough stew, would be willing to argue with the rest of world in his name? He held her gaze. "Maybe we should end this. Whilst we can."

Her features twisted. "No, I—"

He grabbed up the linen and tossed it at her. "Cover yourself."

She fumbled with the linen. "Konstantin—"

"I am done feeling like a criminal in all aspects of my life. I have to build something for myself, Cecilia. Something I have never allowed myself to do given the way I was raised. My financial circumstances have changed, and with it, an opportunity to do more with my life. I haven't told you, but when I get to London, I will be worth more than any man in your circle. I will be a wealthy man able to afford everything and anything I want."

She clutched the linen.

"I rescued a good man who is being overly generous." He braced himself. "I have enjoyed our time together and I want to get to know you more. Am I asking too much too soon?"

A breath escaped her. She raked her long hair away from her face with both hands and groaned. "London isn't like Russia, Konstantin. I have to think about my daughters. People would judge them if we became publicly involved. It would be a mess."

His eyes burned hearing her say it. "I understand." He didn't. "I want more and you want less."

She pressed her hand against her mouth. "You are going to make me cry."

He didn't look at her. "I would rather you not."

She grew quiet.

If only she would fight for him. If only. He would have astounded her by giving her the world. "We have a stagecoach to board." He pushed out a breath, walked past her and grabbed up his trousers from the floor, yanking them on. Buttoning his trousers, he stalked over to the chair, knowing he had to check the time. Digging into the inner pocket of his coat, he dragged out his watch and flipped open the silver lid.

He froze. In the name of God. It was almost a quarter to noon. "Get dressed. The coach leaves in twenty minutes. And if we do not board it, we are stranded here for another week."

She stumbled against the linen and scrambled over to her clothing draped on the other chair before the hearth. Dropping the linen, she fumbled to get her chemise on but only flailed.

He skidded over to her clothing and started grabbing it piece by piece. He tugged her chemise down to help her.

She glanced back at him from over her shoulder. "I know everything happened so quickly between us, but—"

"There is no need to say anything more. It is what it is. Now hold still and let me focus." He couldn't have her talking. He just couldn't.

He adjusted the corset onto her body, bringing it together and laced it as fast as he could. At one point, he finally stopped thinking and did what he needed to do to get her and him dressed. So she could become a lady again. And he could become the male commoner with a criminal past who had stupidly forgotten to remember that despite his impending one hundred thousand, he was only as good as his muddy boots.

An hour later

She knew she should have sat by the window.

Pressed in between two young females with straw bonnets tied over their braided heads, who kept adjusting and re-adjusting their overly large twig baskets filled with their belongings, Cecilia let out a soft breath. She tried to ignore that each basket dug into each of her thighs through her gown.

The sway of the stagecoach and the constant clattering of wheels was also giving Cecilia a nauseating headache. All she could think about was that she was already pregnant. Never mind how it came about, or what people would do or say, another babe was not exactly what she had in mind for herself at forty.

It was mind rattling. Since her husband's death, she had done nothing but tend to her children and their lives. Not once had she actually considered commencing life anew for herself with the sort of man she *really* wanted. Tightening her hold on her empty beaded reticule, which in her opinion, was now merely vanity, she veered her gaze to Konstantin.

He sat wedged between two much shorter men in the seat opposite her own, his wool cap slung low over his forehead. He stared out grudgingly toward the windows as passing muddy fields and budding trees blurred by.

She regretted hurting him by proposing he was only worth midnight visits. But there was no setting aside the truth. He wasn't the sort of man she *could* introduce to her circle. She didn't care what it would do to her and her name. But she did have her girls to think about. Her Giselle would have her coming out in two years.

One of the young women beside her, who couldn't have been more than nineteen, shifted, digging the twig basket into Cecilia's thigh even harder.

Cecilia winced against the sharp, twisting poke.

The young blond paused and glanced toward Konstantin with large blue eyes, her ungloved fingers tightening around the basket. She pinched her lips, quietly observing him. After a long moment, Cecilia noted with a quick sidelong glance, that the young woman had tugged her shawl down and away from her shoulders to better display her calico gown and her décolletage.

Cecilia tightened her lips.

The young woman sat up a touch higher on the seat, bumping Cecilia with the basket again and continued to pertly watch Konstantin as if hoping he would notice her. She tugged down her décolletage a touch lower, to better showcase the upper curve of her breasts.

Cecilia considered taking the woman's basket and pulling it over that braided head. But that, of course, would have been something her daughters would have done.

Konstantin paused and glanced toward the woman, as if sensing he was being watched.

The young woman smiled brightly.

Konstantin inclined his head but said nothing.

The young woman, still smiling, casually rummaged through her large basket, saying something to the other female beside Cecilia.

The other young woman, who also couldn't have been more than nineteen, responded with a flurry of Russian and rummaged through her own basket set on her lap.

Six hours of this was going to kill her.

Yarn and wooden needles were pulled out in rehearsed unison. It was as if these two were about to demonstrate their household skills before a man.

They blithely chatted a bit louder than what was necessary and stretched the wool yarn with long arm movements that nudged and shook Cecilia as they wound up spiraling yarn that kept falling toward the floor.

All Cecilia could see was yarn and hands, yarn and hands.

Soon, it was all over their baskets, their hands and the floor of the carriage.

Two of the other men in the stagecoach, along with Konstantin, now stared.

The young blond panicked and tried to gather everything that had fallen. It only unraveled more.

In exasperation, Cecilia glanced toward each of the young women. They reminded her of herself at their age. Wanting so desperately to impress the right man but unable to. It would seem no matter what country a woman was in, the problems were all the same.

Setting her reticule onto her lap with a sigh, Cecilia reached over to the blond beside her in a motherly attempt to help the poor girl. Cecilia tugged the half-unraveled bundled from the girl's hands and expertly wound the entire yarn back onto its bundle.

The young woman paused and watched Cecilia. Within moments, Cecilia was done. She handed it back to the blond and then grabbed up the brunette's unraveled bundle and wound that one, too, before handing it back.

Konstantin shifted hard in the seat across from them.

Cecilia snapped her gaze toward him.

He stared, his green eyes holding hers.

Her stomach flipped knowing he'd been watching her.

The young blond sat up. As if having finally found her opportunity, she quickly leaned forward in her seat and asked Konstantin something.

Konstantin paused and also leaned forward, answering her in a husky tone.

Cecilia gripped her reticule hard. In that moment, she realized something God awful. That she, Lady Cecilia Evangeline Stone, was actually jealous of a nineteen-year-old girl. It was stupid and it was wrong. She considered herself well-balanced in mind and in character. But apparently, she was neither. And why would she be? She had allowed a man to take over her body and her mind within a few short breaths of meeting him. What rational woman did that?

The blond glanced toward Cecilia and quietly commenced knitting.

Cecilia gripped her reticule even harder. She was being discussed.

She knew it. "What did she say?"

Konstantin leaned back against the seat between the two shorter men who were reading newspapers. Intently searching Cecilia's face, he said, "She asked if you were my mother." With that, he slung his cap low, hiding his eyes and pretended to go to sleep without announcing what his reply was to the girl.

Cecilia almost flung her reticule at him from where she sat, but knew he wasn't to blame for any of this. She was. And fight it though she may, deep in her heart she knew she wasn't ready to let him go.

She had never fought for anything but herself and her girls and her son. But maybe it was time to change that. Maybe it was time to become the sort of woman she had always wanted to be and not the sort of woman society expected her to be.

LESSON SEVEN

Once you fully understand the nuances of your lover's life,

only then can you begin to understand why they resist.

-The School of Gallantry

Saint Petersburg

Evening

As the stagecoach pulled up to the bustle of the gas lit theatre where Konstantin knew it was best place to inquire about her son, Konstantin glanced toward the now empty seats where Cecilia still slept, tucked into the corner of the upholstered seat in exhaustion.

His chest tightened. They had hardly spoken more than a few superficial words during travel. With so many people in the carriage, it had been difficult.

Knowing she needed to rest after sitting seven full hours between two chatty young women who had talked the *entire* way, he exited the coach quietly.

Once outside, Konstantin leaned toward the driver. "I will pay our fare in full upon my return. I ask that you please let her sleep. I will return shortly."

The driver inclined his head. "I will wait here and ensure no one gets on the coach. The amount due to me, sir, is thirty rubles."

"Thank you. I will return shortly." Konstantin adjusted his coat and blowing out a breath, jogged through the gathering crowds that led into the theatre. Painted posters of Miss Katerinochkin seductively peering out from a red velvet curtain were plastered on every wall. He was relieved there was a performance happening tonight. He'd most likely be able to locate Cecilia's son sooner with Miss Katerinochkin about.

He veered past others and strode toward the vast entryway leading inside. Walking into the lamp-lit quarters of the carpeted theatre, the strong, tangy smell of cigars and the heavy scent of mulled wine greeted him as men and women of all caliber lingered in the main entrance, waiting admittance into their assigned boxes or seats.

His eyes darted over to a balding man dressed in a black buttoned coat and an overly starched white cravat that sat behind an open glass window leading into a small secretarial-like room. The man was gathering papers scattered before him and filling mail slots beside him.

"Good-evening, sir," he called out, quickly approaching. "I require assistance."

"Of course," the balding man declared. "How might I be of service to you, sir?"

Konstantin removed his wool cap, smoothing the sides of his hair and leaned against the ledge of the open window. "I am looking for a gentleman by the name of Lord Stone. Would you happen to know anything of his whereabouts? From my understanding, he and—"

"Do you have an appointment?" The man lifted both bushy brows.

"An appointment? What do I need an appointment for?"

"To see Lord Stone, of course. So you may discuss whatever business you may have."

Konstantin blinked. "The man is here? In the theatre?"

"Yes, sir. He is always here during performances."

Thank God. "Can I see him?"

"If you have no appointment, 'tis best you arrange for one." The man grabbed a ledger. After scanning its pages, he dipped a quill into ink. "He is available in two weeks. May 15th. Thursday."

"Two weeks? No. I need to see him now." Before he got anymore attached to a woman who was never supposed to have been part of his life.

The man sighed and lowered the quill. "Please try to understand that with him being the owner of the theatre, his lordship is incredibly occupied."

Owner of the theatre? Holy— Owning a theatre was ludicrously expensive. Apparently, Cecilia *had* married well. Though she somehow failed to mention her son *owned* the theatre. "His mother needs to see him at once. Might I speak to him?"

The man slowly put away the quill. "From my understanding, Lady Stone is not due to arrive for another week." He didn't sound in the least bit interested in helping.

Konstantin leaned toward him, resting an elbow on the edge of the counter and tried to keep his voice civil. "You may want to inform Lord Stone that his mother has arrived *ahead* of schedule thanks to me."

The man lifted his round chin slightly. "And who are you, sir?"

Konstantin sighed. He probably shouldn't attach 'lover' to any of this. "I am an acquaintance. And I am asking that you cooperate. Or when I do find Lord Stone, I will send him straight to you so you might explain to the man why his mother was never given any assistance."

The balding man leaned forward and looked past him. "There is no need for that, sir. I was simply asked not to disturb Lord Stone tonight. He is incredibly busy tending to theatre matters. But seeing this concerns his mother, I will direct you to where he is." He hesitated and added, "I will do so right now."

Konstantin patted the counter. "Thank you, sir."

"I am always at the service of Lord Stone's family. Please wait where you are. I will be out shortly." The man slid the glass window shut and latched it. Organizing a few more papers, he left the small room through a back door and eventually re-appeared around a far corner. The balding man wagged a hand, signaling Konstantin to follow.

Konstantin followed the balding man down a narrow side corridor that led into a hidden small foyer with black and white marble tiles. Elegant, round alcoves displayed a series of bronze and white statuettes propped on Roman-like columns.

He paused in the middle of the foyer.

Female voices echoed in the distance as his eyes followed the decorative black iron railing and stairs that trailed alongside one wall, squared up toward another and disappeared altogether upstairs.

The man went up. "This way, sir."

Konstantin mounted the stairs. Once on the second floor, various female voices lilted from down the hall. Laughter and the clanging of cymbals in another part of the theatre filled the air.

"Lord Stone is inside." The man gestured toward the direction of an open door. "I will be downstairs should you need anything else."

"Thank you." Konstantin walked through the tall doorway and into a small, dignified drawing room with arched ceilings that displayed lace and ribbon plasterwork, gilded accents, and powder blue walls. Though the room wasn't well-lit, everything was still visible enough to hold a sense of coziness that was reflected in the burning hearth and the glow of gilded sconces lining the powder blue walls.

He paused at finding a group of eight scantily clad women in silk robes gathered around a good-looking dark-haired gentleman in black formal evening attire. The young gentleman lounged on a red velvet chaise with a lit Havana cigar between straight white teeth and held a glass of port in one hand, whilst his other hand rested comfortably on the derriere of a busty brunette who was clearly *not* Miss Katerinochkin.

So much for the boy being shy.

The eight women gathered around him seemed intimately comfortable with Lord Stone as they blithely chatted to him in broken English and leaned in closer, some of them allowing their bare white shoulders to purposefully peer through their barely affixed robes. One of the women was sliding a slow hand up Lord Stone's thigh, while another played with the flap of his trousers.

If that had been his son, lounging like some sheik in a harem, treating women like they were all pieces of candied ginger to be chewed and spit out, he'd be caning the boy's ass until there was nothing left to cane. As his father used to always say, one woman at a time.

Konstantin stalked toward them and sat in an empty plush chair across from them. He yanked his wool cap back onto his head to free his hands and cleared his throat to ensure they knew he was in the room.

Lord Stone and his gaggle of females paused and turned their attention, one by one, in Konstantin's direction. Lord Stone handed off his port to one of the women and scrambled up, re-buttoning his trousers. "You had better have a bloody good reason for being here," he tossed out in Russian. "Who let you in?"

Konstantin lifted a curt hand in return greeting and dryly said in schoolroom English, "I hate to interrupt what appears to be *very* serious theatre business, Lord Stone, but I am asking that you evacuate all of these women before your mother sees the sort of son she raised."

Lord Stone jumped up onto polished booted feet, removing the lit cigar from his lips. His dark eyes, that matched Cecilia's right down to the color, darted toward the open doorway. "My mother is here? At the theatre?"

Konstantin rose and straightened to his full height that, to his surprise, matched the boy's own. "Yes. Shall I call her in for you?"

Lord Stone winced and dashed out the smoldering cigar into a nearby crystal ash pan, his dark tonic hair falling from its swept back hold and into his eyes. "No, no. Don't. She would cane me if she saw any of this. I will go to her." He waved off all eight women and said in harried Russian, "Put some clothes on! My mother is here!"

The women giggled and one by one, disappeared with the flap of silk robes out into the corridor and from sight.

Lord Stone smoothed his silk cravat with a bare hand, a ruby and gold ring glinting from his finger and paused. Slowly rounding Konstantin, he scanned Konstantin's appearance from boot to wool cap and then asked in a clipped, overly English tone, "Are you the driver? How much do I owe you?"

Konstantin almost punched the youth out. "No. I am not the driver. I am merely an acquaintance of hers." Konstantin widened his stance. "Your mother is exhausted and is currently asleep in the stagecoach outside. I thought you should know she was drugged by her travelling companion and then robbed of her money and trunks and was left witless on a random coach without any travelling papers."

Lord Stone's eyes widened. "Jesus Christ. Is she all right?" he demanded.

"No harm came to her."

A shaky breath escaped the youth. "Where is she?" He glanced toward the doorway. "Is the stagecoach in the front or the back of the theatre?"

Konstantin shifted his jaw. "Before I tell you where she is, might I ask how things are progressing between you and Miss Katerinochkin? Does she know anything about these women whose derrieres you openly pat? Or do you plan on telling her *after* the wedding?"

Lord Stone swung back to him, his youthful but masculine features tightening. "There is no wedding. I called it off."

"I am very sorry to hear it. It appears your mother left behind all of your sisters and traveled a long way for nothing."

Lord Stone's dark brows flickered. "Who are you?"

Konstantin inclined his head. "Mister Levin."

"No. Who are you to my mother?"

Maybe he *should* have pretended to be the driver. "A friend."

"That sounds incredibly ambiguous, Mr. Levin." Lord Stone veered in close. "How did you know about my engagement? Or that I have sisters? Knowing such private details about my family insinuates there is an intimacy between you and my mother. Am I wrong in assuming that?"

Konstantin said nothing. This was Cecilia's son. What was he supposed to say? That he seduced his mother?

Lord Stone flexed his hands. "London isn't Russia, Mr. Levin. In London, women are *ostracized for life* for associating with the wrong men. And whilst I do not mean to judge you based on what I see, if any disreputable rumors surfaced regarding my mother, every single one of my sisters, who have yet to debut, would be turned away from every respectable match and every respectable home in London. You would be destroying their lives. Are you aware of that?"

Konstantin's throat worked mutely. He hadn't really thought about Cecilia's daughters or how this would affect them. Of course Cecilia would choose her daughters over him. It was the right thing to do. It was the only thing to do. And the pompous ass that he was, he had wanted her to fight for him. Jesus.

It was time to bury this. He owed Cecilia that much. "You mistake our association, sir. I helped your mother get into Saint Petersburg. Nothing more. She was stranded, after being robbed and had no money or a way of finding you because the letter with your address was taken along with everything else. I helped her find you."

Lord Stone's features stilled. "Is she safe? That is all I want to know."

"Yes," Konstantin said in strained tone. "Your mother is safe."

"She had better be, Mr. Levin. For your sake, she had better be."

He liked that the boy was protective of his mother. It reminded him a lot of himself. When he still had his mother. Konstantin swallowed. He missed his hard-eyed mama. He missed being able to sit down at her linen-covered table in that sunlit room of hers decorated with dried flowers where every known criminal always gathered for her food. He missed how she would slap his hands to keep him from eating her almond cake before it could be properly served and then give him the biggest slice out of all the guests to make up for the slaps. He missed watching her arrange every tea cup on every plate, as if needing them to be perfectly aligned before he or any man could raise it to their lips. That was shortly before she suffered from an illness no doctor could cure. Tough as she was, she had smiled up at him through her pain and sweat to the end.

He couldn't help but wonder what she would say about him falling for an older aristocratic woman with four children. She always said things the way they needed to be said. She would have probably shaken her greying head and fussed the way she always did, '*You are too much like your father. Midnight is an illusion. It isn't real.*'

Lord Stone turned and strode over to a small writing desk. Pulling out a leather pocketbook, he strode back and unfolded it. He tugged out all of the crisp bank notes and held them out. "A thousand rubles, sir. For assisting my mother. She means the world to me."

Konstantin pushed away the youth's hand and the bank notes. "Put that away. I have no need for it."

Lord Stone held it back toward him. "Take it. I have no doubt my mother would wish to show you her appreciation."

Konstantin shook his head, trying to remain calm at the mention of Cecilia. "No. I have to go."

Lord Stone lowered his hand, searching his face. "Do you need a place to stay?"

He was not spending another night or another breath anywhere near Cecilia. Or he'd never get out. "No. Thank you. I have a place to stay. I used to live in Saint Petersburg and know countless people." None of them worked legally but they were good men. He only ever associated with the good ones.

"Are you certain?"

God. The boy looked so much like Cecilia. The boy had her dark, soulful eyes. "Quite."

Lord Stone shoved his money back into the pocketbook.

Konstantin hooked his thumbs on his coat pockets. "I should go. I am off to London." He strode toward the door and then called out over his shoulder, "Are you coming? Your mother is in the coach outside."

Lord Stone jogged after him and in between their quick strides down the corridor kept glancing toward him. "So you live in London?"

"No. I am moving to London for a small while until I decide what to do next."

"And where will you be living whilst there?"

What the hell was this? "Why do you want to know?"

"Because I may have to hunt you down if I discover you're lying to me about anything."

"Is that a threat?"

"I want an address, Mr. Levin. I don't trust you. It's as simple as that."

"Thirty-two Belgrave Square. Visit anytime."

Lord Stone jerked to a halt.

Konstantin didn't even bother to look back. He kept walking.

Lord Stone jogged up and fell into stride again beside him. He said nothing.

Konstantin was grateful.

They rounded out of the corridor, down the stairs and back toward the lobby of the theatre where people were now making their way into the auditorium behind them. He made his way through the entrance doors and back out into the foggy night air.

Pulling thirty rubles from his pocket, and unfolding the bank notes, Konstantin gestured toward the stagecoach that was now in sight beyond the crowds they began weaving through. "Let me pay the driver and grab my satchel." Konstantin veered to a halt before the coach's window, realizing Cecilia's dark head was still peacefully tucked against the seat inside in exhausted slumber.

He swallowed. He honestly didn't have it in him to say farewell knowing he wouldn't see her again. What more was there to say? He wanted more for her and her girls and he wanted more for himself. Cecilia made him realize something he'd never fully acknowledged until now. That by settling for less, he became less. Like his father. He had to start wanting more in life. Even if it meant giving up more.

He turned and held out a quick hand, keeping Lord Stone from approaching the coach. "Can you not wake your mother until after I am gone? I am not very good at farewells." Trying to remain calm, knowing he would never see his Cecilia again, Konstantin said, "After I leave, could you please convey one last message to her?"

"Of course. What should I tell her?"

"Tell her it was an honor." With that, he held up the thirty rubles he owed the driver and yanked his sack off the back of the coach. Putting up a quick hand in farewell to Cecilia's son, Konstantin strode toward the direction of the street and into the foggy night.

Every step hurt. But he was proud of himself. He was proud knowing he wasn't leaving her in the name of bitterness or anger or defiance. He was leaving in honor of what they had shared. He was leaving in honor of her girls, like a respectable, good man would. Above all, he was leaving in honor of a beautiful, beautiful woman, whom he would yearn for and think about, for many, many years to come.

LESSON EIGHT

We seldom give any thought as to how many times our
heart beats in a single minute until we are forced to count.

-The School of Gallantry

The slamming open of the carriage door, the sound of endless voices and the sway of the coach as if someone were getting on startled Cecilia out of the deep sleep she had succumbed to. She sat up, a breath escaping her and glanced toward the seat where Konstantin had sat throughout their journey.

She paused.

Her son, John, sat across from her. He scanned her well-mussed appearance, his features twisting. "I heard you were robbed. Are you all right?" Emotion overtook his face.

Tears pricked her eyes at seeing that manly face. He looked so much older. It had been two years since he had taken off to Russia. "John." She scrambled toward him and falling into the seat beside him, grabbed his tonic-brushed, dark head and pressed him against herself. She kissed the warmth of his cheek several times and then his head several times, realizing he smelled of cigars. She paused. Gone was the boy who smelled of the fields he used to run in. "Tell me you didn't commence smoking cigars like your father."

"I can assure you, I have far better taste in cigars than he did."

She sighed. "Drat you." She sighed again and held him tighter. "Your sisters are beyond miserable without you."

He smirked. "Good. I miss them too."

"I had several letters from all of them to give to you, but everything was taken." She groaned. "All of my money, my trunks. Everything."

His features sobered. "I know. I'm sorry. I'm so sorry you had to—" John tightened his hold and rocked her. After a long quiet moment he said miserably, "I'm not getting married, Mama. So you needn't worry. I know you didn't approve. And I don't blame you."

Cecilia pulled away from him, grabbing at his hands. She searched his face, noting that he wasn't looking at her. All she knew was he was miserable. "What happened?"

He didn't meet her gaze. "Tatiana got involved with some Spanish count. It had been going on for months. She was merely using me to pay off debts."

Cecilia's stomach dropped. "Oh, John. I'm so sorry."

He shrugged. "Not quite as sorry as I am knowing you came all this way for nothing. Well over a month of travel by boat and coach only for you to be robbed." He sighed. "Even worse, I bought the theatre Tatiana performs in. It cost me ten thousand."

She gasped. "*What*?"

His hand hit the seat beside him twice. "I know, I know. It was stupid. I was trying to invest in her career. Know, however, that the theatre is set to be sold next week at a good price and I'm going home with you. I'm done here."

Her eyes widened and she felt as if her chest were about to burst knowing he was coming back home. Home. Where he belonged. She grabbed his face again and kissed his cheek hard. Twice. "I never sold your townhome or your membership at the club. A part of me *knew* you would come back."

"I'm glad you didn't sell either." A breath escaped him. "It's time I grow up. I have to…" He skimmed her appearance and groaned. "Jesus. Mother. Even the pins in your hair are gone. Are you certain you're all right?"

Cecilia pinched her lips and smoothed her loose hair back and away from her face with quaking hands. She couldn't find any of the pins after she and Konstantin had rushed out of the inn practically half-dressed in an attempt to catch their coach.

She paused, realizing Konstantin wasn't in the carriage. She turned against the seat and shifted toward the open door of the carriage where people passed by outside in harried steps. Her heart pounded. "Where is Mr. Levin?"

John shifted toward her. "He left. I offered him money and a place to stay given what he did for you, but he refused."

Cecilia's breaths unevenly escaped her in disbelief. No. No, no, no. She hadn't even had a chance to— Oh God. This was not what she wanted. "You let him leave? Without waking me up?!"

He angled toward her, searching her face. "He lied to me. You and he are involved. Aren't you?"

Her cheeks felt like fire. "I didn't mean for us to get involved."

He glared. "But you did."

"Cease glaring at me as if I were two."

"Dearest God. Did you and he…?" He whistled between his teeth and rolled his hand so as not to say the actual word.

"Enough, John. That is not for you to know."

John dropped his hand into his lap with a smack. He leaned in close. "I am not about to lecture a forty-year-old woman, who also happens to be my mother, but you had best leave what happened between you and him buried here in Russia. Do you understand? Russia is one thing. The people abide by their own passions and no one blinks. But London? They don't know *anything* about passions. They punish you for them. You know that. In my opinion, he did the right thing by leaving. You have to let him go. You have to."

Her lips parted, still in disbelief that Konstantin had walked out of her life. "Did he say anything when he left?" She could scarcely say it aloud. "Anything at all?"

He sighed. "He said it was an honor and nothing more. He wanted to leave and even asked I not wake you."

Her heart sank straight down to her booted feet. For him to have left without telling her good-bye meant she'd hurt him. She had said all of the wrong things. Things she wished she had never said. She paused. Maybe he hadn't gone far. Maybe—

Cecilia scrambled past John. Gathering her skirts, she stumbled down the iron steps and onto the pavement. She spun toward her left and right, scanning all of the faces and buildings blurring into shadows and fog and gas lamps. "Which way did he go, John? I have to find him!"

John sat in the carriage, clearly astounded.

She jerked toward him, her heart pounding. "John, for heaven's sake, I have to find him!"

He rose from the seat. Jumping out of the stagecoach with a solid thud of his boots, he adjusted his coat and rounded toward her. "He left well over ten minutes ago."

Oh, God. She clasped a shaky hand against her mouth, realizing Konstantin, her Konstantin, was gone. Forever. Because of her.

John softened his tone. "'Tis better this way."

She closed her eyes in disbelief. "No," she whispered, eventually re-opening her eyes. "This isn't what I wanted. It feels wrong. Letting him disappear from my life feels wrong."

He gaped. "*Wrong*? He allowed your good name to be tainted by permitting an association that could have destroyed you both."

"So says the man who wanted to marry a Russian actress twenty some years older than himself," she tossed back. "Do you think I came out here to celebrate with you? I came to stop the wedding. Only to find there is none!"

He winced and scrubbed his head. "I know, I know, I wanted more for myself than what London had to offer and tried to…" He grabbed her and pressed her against himself. "I'm sorry. If I hadn't come here, if I hadn't met Tatiana, you wouldn't have…" He pressed her harder against himself. "Try not to let this Russian hurt you. He wasn't worthy of you. Christ, he wasn't even properly dressed or—"

She flung away his arms in disbelief. "For shame, John, to be judging a man based on his appearance. For shame. Need I remind you, your father was well dressed. He was so well dressed he couldn't even bring himself to wrinkle his thirty pound trousers in the name of putting his own children onto his lap when they came to him. He was so well dressed that when you fell into that lake as a boy and were drowning, he yelled for the governess to jump in. *The governess*! She and I were the ones who jumped in after you first before he realized two women in the water made him look the fool that he was."

Tears blinded her, remembering that day. "I don't want or need that sort of refinement, John. What I want and need is someone willing to save *me*. I need someone willing to sleep in a wooden chair for *me*. I need someone willing to give me his food even when he has none. That is what I need. And this man did that, John. He put my needs before his own every single time. He did more for me these past two days than your father did his entire life!"

John grew quiet.

A tear unexpectedly spilled down her cheek. She swiped it away with a quaking hand, knowing people were weaving around them. Fortunately, it was Russia and nobody understood a word of what she said. "As frightening as it was to have been robbed and left stranded in a random coach in the middle of Russia, it was the best thing to have ever happened to me. *He* was the best thing to have happened to me." Her voice cracked with emotion, knowing she would never get the chance to tell Konstantin that.

Turning toward the crowds around them, she almost sobbed. Running down empty streets at night would yield nothing but the reality that he was gone. "I'm not ready to let him go," she choked out, tears stinging her eyes. "I told him I was, but I'm not. I'm not."

John searched her face and slowly dragged a rigid hand across his mouth. "Are you telling me you're in love with him?"

She sniffed miserably. "I haven't known him long enough to say that, but he was amazing, John. As a person and as a man. He was amazing."

John dropped his hand to his side. "How amazing?"

"Amazing enough to hang my name on."

"Christ." He blew out a breath. "I…he gave me an address of where he'd be staying in London. I insisted on it before he left."

Her heart almost stopped. "What? You got an address?"

"Yes. I got an address."

She grabbed his face and kissed him twice. "Oh, thank God for you! Thank God you—"

"Mother." He rigidly pulled away and searched her face.

She paused, sensing he was about to announce something she wasn't ready to hear. "What? What is it?"

"The address he gave me is 32 Belgrave Square. Did you not know that?"

Every inch of her skin prickled with gooseflesh as Konstantin's words chimed in her head. '*As my father always used to say, even if you do not believe in destiny, you will in time. Because everything happens for a reason. Which means, we will not be able to escape whatever destiny has planned. Even if we want to.*'

"Dearest Lord," she rasped. "Destiny is real."

John drew his brows together. "What?"

She set a trembling hand to her throat. "Heaven keep me from fainting, John. What are the odds that Mr. Levin would give an address that is right next door to my own home? I knew the grand old house had been let to someone before I left for Russia, I simply never inquired as to who it was."

Lord above. There was no saving them now.

LESSON NINE

Once upon a time, gentlemen, even I failed to become the woman

I wanted to be. 'Tis no shame in admitting you have failed.

There is only shame in admitting you have not tried.

-The School of Gallantry

August 28th, early evening

London, England - 32 Belgrave Square

Steady footsteps echoed in the corridor outside. *His* footsteps.

Konstantin rose from the walnut encased burgundy sofa, his eyes darting to the closed doors of the study he'd been ushered into twenty minutes earlier. Konstantin blew out an exhausted breath, praying to God the man didn't announce he had changed his mind and that Konstantin should get back on a coach and boat and go back to Russia.

The doors of the study slammed open against the oak paneled walls, shaking the large portraits and mirrors hanging throughout the room. The lit candles flickered, sending disfigured shadows wavering across the high, crown molded ceilings.

A tall figure with silvery-steel colored hair dressed in black, right down to leather riding boots, stood motionless in the doorway. It was Duc de Andelot. His face was, as last time, hidden beneath a well-fitted black velvet mask. Only piercing blue eyes and the lower portion of his mouth and shaven jaw peered through. The visible marring of puckered skin on the left side of that aging jaw below the tied mask hinted at the damage hidden.

"We meet again, my Russian friend," Andelot rumbled out in English. As before, there was a slight French accent but it was barely detectable. "How is your shoulder?"

Konstantin thudded his left shoulder. "It healed well."

"I am infinitely pleased to hear it and I am infinitely pleased you came. Although it took you long enough." The duc smirked. "Did the boat sink and leave you to swim?"

Konstantin smiled and inclined his head. "It might as well have. Russia is not exactly next door, Your Grace. I stayed in Saint Petersburg a bit longer than I had planned." It had been some time since he had laid wreaths on the graves of his parents. He made certain to do that before he left Russia. He had also lingered across the street one night outside Lord Stone's theatre during a performance, hoping to see Cecilia. If only one last time. He never saw her.

A part of him was glad for it.

The yearning had to stop.

The duc entered the room, his movements smooth and ghost-like. A raw, contained power rolled off of those limbs hidden beneath well fitting evening clothes that hinted the older man had spent most of his life boxing and fencing and dueling. "Might I offer you a drink, Levin? Sherry? Cognac? Or are you hungry? Shall I have the chef prepare something for you? Is there anything you wanted? Name it and it is yours."

Anything he wanted? How about Cecilia? He refrained from asking. Konstantin shook his head. "No, thank you. I ate at an inn before coming into London. But I would like to take this moment to thank you for inviting me into a city I have always wanted to see. I only wish I had not arrived at night. I could hardly see anything."

"There will be plenty of time for that. But I should probably warn you London is a bit quiet this time of year. The Season is long over and most homes are vacated by now. I personally prefer it. A man cannot think with crowds of people around him. So tell me. How was your journey?"

"I spent most of my time hanging over the railing of the boat, releasing my innards through my nose and my mouth. Other than that…it was pleasant." Konstantin hesitated and cleared his throat. "I also wish to thank you, Your Grace. I really do. I am still a bit overwhelmed and still do not believe I deserve it. I am asking that you reduce the amount. I hardly think—"

Andelot snapped up a scarred hand. "There is no need for us to discuss this. It is done. The money will be in your hands by the end of this week and all I ask is that you not let others know where the money came from. We are merely good comrades and nothing more."

"But the amount is—"

"The amount is respectable. Are you telling me my life is worth less?"

Konstantin blinked. "No, I—"

"I am a generous man, Levin. Let us leave it at that. I have endured a lot and never give any less than what I believe a man deserves." He paused before Konstantin and lingered, staring him down through the slits of his mask. He gestured rigidly toward Konstantin's throat that was exposed. "What is this? Where is your cravat? You did this last time."

Konstantin's hand jumped to his bare throat, grazing his linen shirt. "I never wear cravats. Unless I am required to."

The duc glared. "You cannot step out into public looking like you have lived in a cave all your life. 'Tis an insult to those who are forced to look upon you. Tomorrow, you are going straight to my tailor to conduct measurements for the sort of clothing a man like you should be wearing. Because if it looks cheap, it is cheap. And no one bows to cheap."

Andelot leaned in, the scent of leather and cologne wafting toward the air between them and adjusted the lapel of Konstantin's coat. The duc sighed. "I regret not giving you money sooner. When you awake tomorrow, my valet will properly shave you. With the amount of money going into your pocket, Levin, 'tis your duty to represent yourself well. Or no one will take you seriously."

Konstantin swiped his hand across his now ten-day-old beard. He knew he should have shaved at the last inn. "Forgive me. I get lazy sometimes."

"I can see that." Andelot glanced toward the clock on the mantelpiece. "I do not wish to be rude, but I have an appointment to keep. Are you tired? Or are you up for joining me?"

"I would not be imposing?"

"No." Andelot turned and strode toward one of the bookshelves. He ran a hand across the bindings of all the leather books before stopping and yanking one out. He carried it over and held it out. "Take this for me."

Konstantin hesitated and slid the book from the man's scarred hand. It was Voltaire. The gold lettering on the leather binding read in English *Candide: or The Optimist*. Turning it toward himself, Konstantin's brows came together. The leather binding was warped and appeared to be heavily damaged by age. "This has certainly seen a lot of use."

"Good books usually do." The duc strode by. "Come. And bring Voltaire with you."

"Where are we going?"

Duc de Andelot paused, as if the question had affected him. He lingered, not looking at anything in particular. "I usually go alone, but I trust you. And truth be told, I would rather not be alone tonight."

When their carriage paused in the shadows outside a very respectable-looking townhome, outside the light of surrounding gaslights, the duc gestured toward the book with his cane. "Read."

Konstantin shifted against the leather upholstered seat of the carriage and swiped up the book beside him. He hesitated. What happened to the so-called appointment? They were stationed alone on the side of a road somewhere in London at ten o'clock at night. It didn't feel right. "Uh…is there a reason you want me to—"

"Start at Part two on page one hundred and three. And above all, handle it with care. That is an original English printing."

Maybe the man's eyes were getting old.

Konstantin cleared his throat, carefully paged to what appeared to be half the book. He found the page and tilted the book toward the dim light of the lantern. "*Part Two. Chapter One. How Candid quitted his companions and what happened to him.*" Interesting. He'd never read Voltaire. He read on. "*We soon became tired of everything in life; riches fatigue the possessor; ambition when satisfied, leaves only remorse behind it; the joys of love are but transient joys; and Candid, made to experience all the vicissitudes of fortune was soon disgusted with cultivating his garden.*"

The duc unlatched the window of the carriage and leaned out, staring up at one of the windows.

Konstantin paused from his reading, realizing the man was no longer listening and inched forward to see what the man was actually looking at.

A silver-haired lady draped in an ivory robe sat beside the window reading by a brightly lit lamp that illuminated her pale face. She adjusted her silver braid over her shoulder.

The duc continued to watch her. Almost never blinking.

Konstantin eyed the man and then the silver-haired lady in the window. "Should we be doing this?"

The duc tapped his lips with a finger and gestured toward the book again, without looking away from the lady or the window. "Read."

Oho. This had trouble smeared all over it. And he wanted no part of it. Konstantin shut the book, slid over to the window and leaned toward the duc. "Let me give you some advice. I have no idea how the English conduct themselves here, but in Russia, men are arrested for these sort of things." He was being serious.

The duc continued to watch the window of the townhouse. "Since when is love a crime, Levin?" he asked, his voice reverberating in the darkness of the carriage.

Konstantin glanced back up to the window. This just got good. He shifted closer. "Who is she?"

The duc gripped his cane tighter, his black leather glove creaking. His eyes had a burning, faraway look. "A whisper of everything I could have had but never will."

Konstantin knew the feeling. "Did she marry someone else?"

"Oh, yes. She married every damn man in sight."

Ooo. She was one of *those*. At least Cecilia hadn't been that. "I am very sorry to hear it."

Andelot hit the end of the cane on the floor of the carriage. "I used to blame her for the path she took. But I have long since come to recognize that it is I who destroyed her by not making an honorable woman of her. I was the one to drape her with her first set of diamonds." Andelot glanced back toward her window again and paused, his cane stilling. An exasperated breath escaped him. Re-latching the carriage window with an agitated swipe of his gloved hand, he settled back against the seat and muttered, "She has retired for the night."

Konstantin surveyed the now dark window.

Andelot lifted his cane and hit the roof of the carriage, commanding the driver to leave.

The driver snapped the reins and the carriage rolled forward, causing Konstantin to sway forward then back as he returned his gaze to the duc.

The man grudgingly lowered his eyes to the gold head of his cane and rigidly tapped the palm of his gloved hand against it. "Next time, I come alone. You talk too much."

Konstantin quirked a brow. "Do you mean to tell me, since coming into London, you have been doing this every night?"

Andelot grunted. "I would never admit to such a thing."

"Which means you have been."

The duc shifted his jaw beneath the mask. "What of it?"

And he thought he was a feather short when it came to women. "Is she the reason why you came to London?"

"Yes."

Konstantin smoothed a hand over the damaged leather binding of the book. "Have you called on her?"

The duc's blue eyes looked piercingly sharp in the light of the moon that drifted in through the window. "I would never."

"Why?"

Lifting his cane up toward his face, Duc de Andelot edged the gold handle across the left side of his tied mask, causing it to shift. "This."

Konstantin couldn't imagine living a life behind a mask and genuinely felt angst for the man.

The duc lowered the cane from his mask.

Konstantin gripped the book hard. "Forgive me for prying, but what actually happened between you and her?"

"Too much." The duc paused, clearly drifting to another place and another time. Those eyes became flat. Unreadable. "When I was much younger, even younger than you are now, I was living two separate lives. One for my father and one for myself. Thérèse was the woman I wanted to marry but couldn't. And when she became pregnant, everything fell apart."

The duc leaned back against the seat, his voice growing ragged, "She refused to accept what our relationship really was. She wanted to be more than a mistress. She wanted us to marry. If I had been anyone else, anyone but third cousin to the King, I would have. But I knew what her life would have turned into and I was trying to keep her safe from my father. She, of course, did not see it that way and not only kept me from seeing my own son, but allowed herself to become the most sought after woman in all of France. God help me, I was so angry with her for becoming the desire of every man. So angry. I did not want my son raised in the world she had involved herself in and even tried to reason with her about what I could offer him, but she was done with me. I wanted to take our son, but I could not rip the boy out of the arms of his mother. She loved him."

Andelot averted his gaze to the dark night beyond the glass window at his shoulder. "I had to let them go." Andelot seethed out a breath. "Then the Revolution swept through Paris turning my beloved France into a nation of savages. Many did not even wait for Robespierre to condemn the elite. They did it themselves. They torched homes until the summer day sky was as dark as night and tossed respectable, titled women into crowds and raped them in public whilst their husbands and children watched. Then they would butcher them all with knives out of their own kitchens. And the worst of it? They did it with pride. They did it whilst waving their blood-spattered flags."

The duc grew quiet. Those lips parted in deep thought before he eventually whispered, "My father was arrested and guillotined. That man brutalized me my entire life – *my entire life* –but even I knew he wasn't deserving of having his head cleaved from his shoulders. The only reason I had not been seized by the tribunal myself was because I was half-British and my mother's entire family from England was petitioning Robespierre in exchange for favors. With what little time I had due to their petitions, I dismissed all of my servants to keep them from harm and harbored aristocrats whose names were on the list of the condemned. I tried planning an escape, but no one was willing to provide us transportation. Not even for the children. All of France had gone mad."

Andelot rubbed at his jaw. "And that was when Thérèse re-appeared in my life. I was…*astounded*. She came to me as if she could hear my prayers drifting through a city filled with smoke. She brought food and arranged for transportation for all of us to leave the country courtesy of one of her *bourgeois* lovers. A part of me wanted to refuse her assistance, but there were others I had to think of. So I allowed for it." Andelot rigidly tapped at his masked face. "As you can see, I barely escaped France. She never saw what was done to me. I made sure of it."

Konstantin numbly held the book between hands that were heavy with disbelief.

Andelot lowered his gaze. Fingering his cane, he murmured, "Long after I came into wealth again, after countless years of toiling and travelling and re-investing what my mother's family in England had generously bequeathed me, I wanted to know if she and my son…needed anything. So I hired men to find them. It took years. Unbeknownst to me, they had left France. Less than a year ago, one of the informants finally had information."

The duc rapidly blinked. "Whilst Thérèse was fine, and I am blessed knowing it, my Henri was dead and had been for a long time. He had died here in England." His voice cracked. "But he left behind a daughter. Maybelle. She lives with Thérèse. And that is why I am here. I want to be part of my granddaughter's life in a way I was unable to be part of Henri's. I simply have not been able to bring myself to knock on that door knowing I have no face and that…men still flock to Thérèse as if she were twenty." Andelot rolled his eyes. "I have heard she associates with an array of men because of some *school* where she gives men advice on-on…*private matters*." He shook his head. "She was always outrageous. She lived for it." His fisted hand hit the seat hard, reverberating through the carriage. He settled himself against the seat. "I need a brandy," he breathed out.

Of course the man needed brandy. "So you have been in London these past few months and still have not called on her or your granddaughter?"

The duc tossed his cane from one hand to the other, back and forth. "My face aside, I genuinely doubt Thérèse would permit me to have an association with Maybelle. She and I did not part on the best of terms."

Konstantin gave him an exasperated look. "How do you know what she will or will not allow if you have not called on her?"

Andelot glanced toward the window and the night beyond.

"Call on her." Konstantin leaned closer. "After everything you survived, including a whole revolution, there is no shame in what you endured or why you wear a mask. Call on her."

Gently tapping the cane against the floor of the carriage, Andelot fixed his sight at nothing in particular. He kept tapping the cane against the floor. "Will you go with me if I call on them?"

Konstantin's chest tightened. "It would be an honor. When do you want to go? Shall we go tomorrow?"

The duc's gaze snapped toward him. "Are you mad? No. The day after. I need time to trim my hair. As do you."

Konstantin bit back a smile. "The trimming of our hair should only take a half hour."

Andelot lowered his chin. "Whilst I appreciate your intentions, I ask that you refrain from any further comments."

Konstantin held up a hand and then set it against his mouth.

LESSON TEN

Passion is a fire you ignite. It can either light a candle

in the darkness or burn down your entire house.

The idea, gentlemen, is not to burn the house.

-The School of Gallantry

Two days later

At the home of Madame de Maitenon

Konstantin dragged a heavy hand through his overly arranged, tonic-fussed hair, which had been trimmed well beyond what he was used to, and warily watched the duc get up and sit in three different upholstered chairs set around the small parlor.

The duc kept shaking his head and openly muttering, "Useless. The woman's taste in comfort is absolutely useless. These furnishings are for the devil."

Konstantin doubted the furnishings were actually the problem.

Andelot eventually decided on a plush green, empire-style chair. He settled into it with a grunting huff and adjusted the red ribbon against his hair that held his mask in place. Crossing his polished riding boots at his ankles, the duc pulled his coat over his waist. "I cannot believe I am doing this. What if she refuses to see me?" Andelot's blue eyes perused the doorway.

Konstantin was beginning to feel nervous for the man. "Everything will be fine. I am certain she will—"

The harried clicking of female heels against the wood floors, that hinted at a half-run, made Konstantin scramble to feet.

The duc uncrossed his boots and sat up but did not rise. "Tell me to calm down."

"Calm down."

"I am trying."

Within moments, a very attractive elderly woman appeared in the doorway of the receiving room, partly out of breath with a cane in hand she leaned against for support. Her thick, silver hair was meticulously arranged in fashionable curls around her pale face. Rose-tinted silk flowers had been woven through her tresses, fashionably matching the shade of her elegant lace gown that showcased a slim, well-corseted frame. A long, expensive-looking string of pearls had been draped from her slender throat to her waist as if to emphasize and draw attention to the sizeable breasts surrounding them. Enigmatic bright blue eyes veered toward the duc.

Konstantin set his hands against his back. Waiting.

They stared wordlessly at each other in the pulsing silence.

If the tension visible between them could have been measured by the size of a flame, those stares would have created a blaze the size of whatever burned the sun.

The duc shifted his jaw beneath the mask. He rose. Adjusting his black leather gloves in the manner a duelist might, he walked toward her, his booted steps steady and determined. He paused directly before her. Widening his muscled stance, the duc gruffly announced, "We will speak in English for the duration of this conversation. Because all things French are dead to me since I left Paris."

She inclined her head toward him, her eyes never once leaving his masked face.

Konstantin cringed for him.

Andelot squared his jaw. "I am here because I wish to see my granddaughter. I wish to have the sort of relationship with her that you never allowed me to have with my son. I know I am asking for a lot, given how we parted, but I believe I have long since grown as a man and am worthy of that honor."

In a sultry French-accented voice, she announced breathily, "I never thought I would see you again." Madame de Maitenon searched the duc's masked face. "You look well for yourself."

The duc snorted and leaned in. "Oh, come, my dear. You need not lie. In answer to the question you have not asked, beneath this mask, half my face is gone."

Madame de Maitenon's expression stilled.

Andelot cleared his throat and tugged on his coat. "Can I meet my granddaughter? Is that at all a possibility?"

She brought her hands together and softly said, "Maybelle has left London with her husband."

The duc's lips parted below the mask. "She is married?"

"Yes. She married quite recently."

"And is she happy with the union?"

"Yes. Very."

"Ah." He half-nodded. "I am glad to hear it." He hesitated. "Who did she marry?"

"His Grace the Duke of Rutherford. They are currently on tour and will be visiting every city in Europe before travelling into Egypt. They are not expected to return for another eight months. When she does arrive back into London, you may call on her. I have no doubt she would want to meet her *grandpére*. As such, I will gladly notify you the moment she returns into town."

A breath escaped the duc. "I would appreciate that."

She nodded. "Where shall I send the missive when she arrives, Gérard? So she might call on you in person?"

The duc hesitated and lowered his chin. "I am living at 32 Belgrave Square. I ask, however, that you do not address me by my birth name. It would give me too much hope."

Madame de Maitenon said nothing.

Andelot set his shoulders and after a few pulsing moments offered, "I thank you for your time, Madame. It was an honor to see you."

Her blue eyes softened. "And you."

Konstantin felt like he was watching something he shouldn't. It felt very *personal*.

Andelot inclined his head. "I wish you a good-day." He rigidly rounded Madame de Maitenon, brushing past her. Disappearing into the corridor, he called out, "Levin, in case you have not noticed, I am leaving." The man opened the door to the entrance and walked out, leaving the door wide open, allowing the afternoon summer air and wind to blow in.

The elderly woman glanced toward Konstantin, tears now visibly gathering in those overwhelmed bright blue eyes. She pursed her lips in a noble attempt not to cry.

Konstantin swallowed. "He needed to see you. He was sitting in a carriage outside your window every night for weeks."

A trembling hand touched her face as she blindly attempted to use the cane to walk to a chair. A sob escaped her.

Konstantin darted toward her and grabbed her hand and her corseted waist, knowing full well she wasn't going to make it. He turned her and gently eased her into the nearest chair, his chest tightening.

She swiped at her tears with one hand, her manicured fingers trembling. She grabbed Konstantin's arm, searching his face with a tear-streaked pale face that flickered with distraught emotion. "Where did the scarring come from? The ones hidden beneath the mask? What happened to him?"

Knowing he owed the woman a measure of comfort, he offered, "He never told me. But he mentioned it happened whilst trying to escape France. After you had arranged transportation for him."

Her hand jumped to her mouth. She closed her eyes, letting another tear slip down her cheek and said through her quaking hand, "Leave me."

He seated himself in a chair beside her. "I will leave once I am assured you are less distressed."

"Whilst kind," she choked out, "that will take more time than you have."

"I have time, Madame," he gently offered. "Do you require anything? Shall I call for one of your servants?"

"No. Thank you." She lowered her hand and sniffed softly. "Might I ask who you are to him?"

He inclined his head. "I am Mr. Levin. I am a friend."

"How long have you known him?"

"A few months. Though most of it was never in his presence."

"You have a heavy accent." Her eyes cut to his. "Are you from

Russia?"

"Yes." Konstantin shifted toward her in his seat. "I wish to assure you that in my country, Andelot is well-known for being everything a man should be. He is a legend in Moscow and is a patron to the poor and all things good. He is incredibly generous. Overly generous. To me and to everyone."

She reached out and delicately touched his arm. "Care for him, Mr. Levin. I am afraid I was always too proud to do right by him. He needs a true friend. The sort he has never had due to his status and upbringing. Promise me you will be a good friend to him."

It was obvious this woman was still in love with Andelot. "I will ensure he stays out of trouble."

"*Merci.*" She removed her hand. She hesitated. "Please tell him I am engaged to be married to Lord Hughes. He needs to know."

Oh, damn. The duc was going to have a fit. And yet…Konstantin sensed she was telling him as if she was hoping Andelot would do something about it. "Pardon my asking, but is there any hope for him?"

She hesitated. "I am not ready to answer that. Thank you for staying, Mr. Levin. It was very kind of you. I am quite well now." Her tone hinted that she wanted to be alone.

"Of course." Konstantin rose and also inclined his head. "Should you require anything, please send a missive to me at 32 Belgrave Square and address it to my name. I should be there for at least another two weeks until I find a place of my own. When I move, I will forward the new address."

"I appreciate your generosity." She swiped away the last of her tears. "*Au revoir*, Mr. Levin."

Konstantin hesitated, nodded and then awkwardly turned, a raw heaviness eating away at his chest and his mind. Once he was outside the townhouse and had gently shut the entrance door the duc had left open, Konstantin hissed out a breath in complete exasperation. He had clearly walked into the middle of a broken affair that had been simmering for well over twenty years.

Jogging down the stairs and landing on the pavement, he paused, realizing the duc was leaning against a lamppost two doors down.

Two younger women with parasols slowed and stared at the duc's masked face.

The duc inclined his head.

They grabbed each other's arms and scurried by with a quick rustle of skirts as if they had just glimpsed the devil.

Konstantin sighed and strode toward the man. Coming to a halt before the man, he confessed, "I think you did well."

Andelot held his gaze, all emotion hidden beneath that black velvet mask. "Why were you in there so long?"

"She was crying. I was trying to console her."

Andelot glanced away. He said nothing.

Konstantin cleared his throat, knowing he needed to say it. "She uh…she wanted me to inform you she is engaged."

Andelot snapped his gaze toward him, his chest rising and falling visibly. "Is that what she said?"

"Yes."

"Jesus." The duc pushed away from the lamppost with a gloved hand and rasped, "Have you ever loved a woman so much that the very breath in your throat is no longer yours but hers?"

Konstantin swallowed. He didn't know about love, but he did know he still couldn't sleep at night without thinking he could smell

Cecilia's perfume on his own skin. And every time he looked at his watch, he thought of how she had lain naked with it, her slim fingers opening and closing the silver lid in playful fascination. "I have come close to knowing it."

"Pray you never do." Andelot veered in close. "Did she tell who she is marrying?"

"A certain Lord Hughes."

Andelot squinted. "Hughes. I know that name. I see him from time to time over at the…" Andelot glanced back toward the townhouse. After a few pulsing moments, he swung away. Striding back to the carriage, whilst tugging on the sleeves of his coat, he said, "I deserve this."

Konstantin huffed out an irked breath. "So you are just going to walk away? You are going to let her marry this Hughes? Is that what you are saying?"

The duc jerked to a halt. He turned and quickly strode back to Konstantin. "I have no face."

Konstantin glared. "There is more to you than your face."

"Such sentiment is beautiful on the tongue but in reality, it is untrue. I have to pay women to bed me."

That was a little too much information. "You should go back and talk to her."

"No." Andelot swung away again and headed back toward the carriage. "She knows where I live."

Konstantin swallowed and genuinely wished he could help Andelot. But who was he to give advice about women? He couldn't even hold onto the woman destiny had handed to him in a coach at midnight.

LESSON ELEVEN

What under heaven's majestic clouds are you waiting for?

-The School of Gallantry

Eight days later – 10:03 p.m.

Next door to 32 Belgrave Square

Konstantin's warm hand smoothed away her pinned curls from her forehead as he leaned in and trailed soft, soft kisses up the curve of her throat. The tips of his calloused fingers gently skimmed down toward her breasts, that lingering touch promising her a lifetime of all things beautiful and romantic. It was pulse-rending. It was genuine. It was divine.

She didn't want to wake up.

But of course she did.

A tap on her shoulder startled her awake. "*Mother*," Abigail's voice whispered down at her. She tapped Cecilia's shoulder a bit more aggressively. "Mother, are you awake?"

No matter how old they got, they still interrupted one's sleep. "I am now," Cecilia murmured, drowsily rolling toward her daughter and dragging the linens with her. She squinted up at Abigail, realizing all three of her daughters were standing at different heights beside her four-poster bed, fully dressed in their morning gowns and satin slippers as if it were two in the afternoon. The eldest, Giselle, regally held up a candle that illuminated their pale, oval faces in a soft, wavering glow of the bedchamber.

Her girls only ever came to her as a group when there was a problem. A serious one. Cecilia sat straight up, her heart pounding. "For heaven's sake, what is it? What happened? Why are all of you dressed?"

"We couldn't sleep," Abigail announced with the firm set of her chin. "We spoke to John. He had mentioned something about a certain gentleman you met in Russia."

Cecilia froze. Oh, no. No, no, no.

"He said this gentleman lives next door beyond the gates and the hedges," Giselle continued for Abigail. "Is that true?"

Cecilia groaned.

Abigail squinted. "Why did you not tell us about this Mr. Levin and how he rescued you?"

She wasn't ready to face this. Not yet. "Can we discuss this in the morning?"

"No. John wouldn't answer any of our questions. What happened in Russia between you and this man? Are you and he friends? Or more than friends? We are old enough to know."

Cecilia wanted to crawl under her bed. But she had never been one to hide her life from theirs. She loved them too much for that. "He and I are more than friends. And I was actually thinking of…calling on him."

All three perked.

Oh, dear. She had just unleashed the romance hounds. "Please. No advice on what I should do."

Giselle waved her free hand toward the closed door behind them, causing the flame on her candle to dance. "The lamps in the house beyond the hedge at 32 are still lit and we can hear the piano being played through our open windows. You should get dressed and see him."

Cecilia almost bit her own hand. She wasn't ready to see him. "I just returned to London seven hours ago. I need to sleep." Which was really a pathetic excuse. She would have already gone over and knocked on that door, but she was scared witless. What if it wasn't the same? What if Konstantin turned her away? What if he had already moved on? She had a million other concerns she couldn't even voice aloud.

They were too young to hear any of it.

Giselle waved about the candleholder in agitation. "There is no need for pretenses, Mama. How can you even sleep knowing he lives right next door? You always complain about being alone and yet here you are ensuring it."

Cecilia cringed. And she thought she was blunt.

Abigail's brown eyes met hers in earnest. "How much do you like this Mr. Levin? A little? Or a lot? Because there is a difference."

It was as if the five months Cecilia had been away, all of her daughters had bloomed into thirty-year-old, well-situated women with advice. "A lot."

Juliet pertly tore off a small piece of the crumpet she held and shoved it into her mouth, her full cheeks rounding. "I suggest you ring for your lady's maid." She chewed majestically several times before adding, "Might I suggest your primrose evening gown and the emeralds you bought last year at auction?"

Cecilia shifted toward them in exasperation. "Have you lost what little you have of your respectable minds? I am *not* calling on him at this time of night. This isn't Russia."

Giselle lowered her chin, her gaze sharpening. "Calling on him during respectable calling hours is nothing short of mundane, Mama. That is what old ladies of the *ton* adhere to. Calling on a man at *this* hour is exciting and proof of your devotion. As long as you keep it to fifteen minutes it might as well be Russia."

Juliet nodded. "I agree. No one of any consequence is even in the neighborhood to take notice of such a visit. Ask the governess. As she always likes to say, the Season is over and the gossips have all gone to the country."

"*Amen for that*," all three girls said in rehearsed unison as if it were some sort of jest.

How was it she had raised not one, not two, but three overly romantic, starry-eyed girls? Where did they learn these things? She certainly never discussed the notion of *romance* with any of them. It was those poetry books the governess insisted on.

"I cannot go to him," Cecilia whined, feeling sixteen and newly dismayed by the reality of a relationship.

"Why not?" Abigail inquired.

"He could have already moved on." With that, she settled back down against the pillow, turned away and closed her eyes, chanting to herself to stay calm.

She felt them lingering. And breathing. And lingering. And breathing.

Satin slippers shifted against the wooden floor in silent defiance, one by one.

She rolled back toward them, opening her eyes.

They stared.

Something told her they weren't going to let her get any sleep.

Giselle eventually said, "If it isn't already obvious, we are rather anxious to meet him. We never thought you would take a liking to a man."

"It would be marvelous to have a new Papa," Juliet added.

Her throat tightened at hearing her daughters wanted a father. It was the first time in seven years they had ever admitted it. A soft breath escaped Cecilia as she slowly sat up. To be young again and not see any of the consequences of what a man and woman faced was precious. But not in the least bit realistic. "Mr. Levin would be treated differently by those in our circle if he and I become involved. We would *all* be treated differently if I accepted him into our lives. People, who may have once invited us to gatherings will turn us away and never speak to us again. And what complicates this entire situation all the more is that Giselle has her coming out in two years."

All three faces flickered as they glanced toward each other with unspoken words.

Giselle sighed. "Do you know why John thought he should marry a Russian actress as opposed to a titled lady? Did he ever tell you?"

Cecilia searched their faces in astonishment. "No. John never—"

"He said after watching you and Father, he wanted more out of life. And when we debut, we will want more, too. We know you gave up a lot for us, and that you did it because you love us, but it's time, Mama. If you like this Mr. Levin a lot, it's time. Whilst our friends are dear to us, you are all the more dearer. You deserve to be happy."

Cecilia blinked rapidly to keep herself from crying. Her son and her girls had convened and were announcing their support. Even knowing

Konstantin wasn't going to be accepted by others.

How she genuinely loved her children for always thinking of her. "Life would be unbearable for all of you if I involve myself with a man outside of our circle," she softly said. "You do know that, yes?"

"If life truly becomes *that* unbearable," Giselle added with the mischievous quirk of her mouth, "we can always move to Russia. None of us would mind. In fact, I hear the Russian men are incredibly dashing. It might prove entertaining to debut in Saint Petersburg at the Russian Court."

"Or America," piped one of the other girls.

Cecilia lowered her chin, trying to decipher if they were serious.

"Yes, Mama," Giselle offered, "we are being *very* serious. Now call on Mr. Levin. If you keep your visit to a respectable fifteen minutes, just as a means of announcing yourself, I can assure you, no harm will come of it."

The girl had a point. "So you think I should I call on him? Despite the hour?"

Juliet sighed. "Are we going to have to pull you out by the legs?"

She didn't need more encouragement than that. Cecilia frantically shoved aside the linens, her heart pounding at the thought of seeing Konstantin again. "I can't believe I'm doing this. Will someone please pull the bell and have Samantha come up at once?"

They grinned in unison.

Abigail bounced her way over to the calling bell and yanked on the braided cord twice. "Done."

Despite those glorious little grins, Cecilia pointed at each and every one of them. "Whilst I am vastly, vastly appreciative of all the support, I am asking that you all find your nightgowns and nightcaps and get some sleep. We will reconvene over breakfast in the morning with any news I may or may not have."

Those grins faded.

Juliet huffed out a breath and stomped a single foot. "You cannot make us suffer like this! We won't get any sleep! Can we not meet him? *Tonight?*"

Cecilia tried to retain her motherly façade of being serious even though she was astounded at seeing Juliet stomp her foot. She hadn't seen that sort of behavior since the girl was six. "You will all meet him only *if* he chooses to accept the challenge of being part of our lives. Which he hasn't yet. We did not part on the best of terms, therefore a courtship or marriage may never come of this. I wish to repeat that. I do not want any of you stitching your hopes to this."

Giselle set the candlestick onto the side table beside the bed. Clasping her hands, she announced in a womanly tone, "I would have to agree with Juliet. Your primrose gown and emeralds will ensure Mr. Levin takes you seriously."

Panic of the unknown scrambled Cecilia's innards.

11:39 p.m.

She had spent so much time preening over her appearance, she was quite sure she had lost what little remained of her rational mind. The amount of emeralds on her ears and her throat and gloved hands were enough to make any former criminal smile in warm welcome. Her only complaint was that Juliet had dabbed her with a bit too much perfume. Especially given the mugginess of the warm summer night. She had no doubt the man would be able to smell her at the door.

Fortunately, every last neighbor in Belgrave Square had long closed their shutters seeing it was late summer and had all travelled to the country, leaving no prying eyes to question what she was about to do. Though she was more than certain everyone would know about it by the end of the week.

Drawing in a long shaky breath, she let it out and twisted the iron knob for the bell beside the massive double oak doors that were barely lit by the lanterns hanging above the entrance.

She had *never* called on a man at such an hour before. Not even for fifteen minutes. It was like being back in Russia.

She glanced toward the lit window on the far right of the house and, as all of her daughters had assessed, there was a beautiful, yearning melody floating from the keys of a pianoforte. It paused, and silence now clung to the night air.

She wondered if it had paused because of her.

The doors eventually fanned open and a footman peered out at her from down his bulbous nose. "Might I be of assistance?"

She hurriedly held out the single calling card she had brought with her. "I apologize for the dreadful hour, sir, but I am in desperate need of seeing Mr. Levin. It is of utmost importance. Utmost." She made sure to emphasize that. "Is he at home?"

The aging butler slipped the card from her fingers with a gloved hand and with a furrowed brow glanced at the card. "Please wait inside so I might inquire for you, Lady Stone." He gestured toward the marble entryway behind him.

"Thank you." She hurried in.

The butler placed her card onto a small silver tray that rested on a side table and swept it up with a gloved hand, taking it into one of the candlelit rooms down the corridor.

There was a murmuring exchange of two male voices.

The butler eventually returned and announced, "Please follow, Lady Stone."

Her heart pounded as she followed him down the corridor. She was ushered into a beautifully decorated receiving room of golden and dark silk hues. The doors closed behind her.

No one was in the grand room.

She swept toward the lamp-lit room that displayed incredibly lavish furnishings of Oriental origins, countless vases and a pianoforte that had five decanters of brandy, two of them already empty as it sat beside a half-empty glass.

She froze, realizing she wasn't alone in the room after all.

A broad shouldered man wearing a black velvet mask, with a blood-red satin ribbon tied around his head of silvery-steel colored hair slowly rose to his full height from the bench at the keys. He stood motionless, only piercing blue eyes and the lower portion of his mouth and shaven jaw peering through. The visible marring of puckered skin on the side of his aging jaw below the tied mask hinted there was considerable damage to his face.

Her lips parted, not at all expecting what she was looking at.

He leaned toward the glass of brandy set on the pianoforte, taking a leisurely swallow and then set it aside. He made his way toward her. "After glimpsing your calling card, I realized we are neighbors. How is it we have never met, Lady Stone?" His voice was regal and smooth, hinting at a bit of French origin, but his words and his stance appeared to be a touch heavy from the brandy. She inclined her head, wondering who this man was to Konstantin. "I was away travelling, sir."

"Sir?" He rumbled out a laugh. "Oh, I like that. Sir." He paused before her, searching her face with a smirk. "I should have left my card for you when I first arrived to Belgrave Square. 'Twas quite…rude of me. The name is Duc de Andelot. Not sir." He reached out a large scarred hand and sloppily took up her gloved hand. "I understand you are here to call on Mr. Levin." He side-kissed the satin of her glove across her knuckles.

A French duc? Was this who Konstantin had rescued? It had to be.

Cecilia watched the man lift her hand to his lips just below that mask and tried not to acknowledge that she could smell the brandy. "Yes, Your Grace. I am here to call on Mr. Levin. I ask that you forgive me for having called you sir. I didn't realize—"

"Think nothing of it. It amused me."

"Is Mr. Levin at home?"

"Yes."

Her breath caught. He was here. Her Konstantin was actually here. She couldn't believe it. Breathe. She tried to breathe. "Might I see him?"

The duc released her hand and strode back to the pianoforte, his staggered steps clearly affected. Pushing back the tails of his black evening coat with one scarred hand, he seated himself on the bench. "I am afraid he retired for the night," he finally said. "He asked not to be disturbed."

"But I have to see him. This cannot wait until morning." She'd go mad.

The duc leaned forward and taking up one of the crystal decanters from the polished surface of the pianoforte before him, filled his empty glass again. He set aside the decanter. "And how is it that you know Levin, Lady Stone? Are you and he…?"

She tried to keep it simple. And respectable. "He nobly assisted me in Russia. I came to thank him for everything he has done for me."

"At this hour?" he pressed, arranging himself more comfortably before the pianoforte.

She inwardly cringed. Why did she feel as if she were suddenly rationalizing her behavior to her father? "Well, I…I just returned from Russia several hours ago and simply could not wait until morning to see him. I am afraid he and I did not part on the best of terms."

He paused. "I think Levin might have mentioned you a few times. But he never gave me a name. Were you the one robbed?"

She blinked. Konstantin had clearly been discussing details about her. "I…yes."

The duc nodded and started to play a haunting melody, his long fingers moving effortlessly across the keys as if brandy had never even touched his veins. He glanced toward her, still playing and said in a low, provocative tone above the music, "You may go to him." Still playing, he flicked his attention to her low cleavage. "He is up the main stairs to the left behind the…*fifth* door on your right. Fifth door. On the right." He leaned in and away from the piano, giving over to the yearning melody and watched her.

She blinked rapidly. For all she knew, this is how masked French men cornered stupid British women in the middle of the night. "I would rather not wander about a house I do not know. Can he be summoned?"

He still watched her and played. "I am asking you to surprise him. He has been unusually quiet and keeps staring at the inscription of his watch. I imagine it has something to do with you."

Her very soul squeezed. "How is he?"

The haunting melody suddenly turned into a harried, playful tune. "Better than I."

This one thought he had a sense of humor. "So he is upstairs?"

That harried tune effortlessly slowed back to the earlier haunting melody. "Yes. Fifth door on the right."

So much for her respectable fifteen minutes. "Thank you, Your Grace." She glanced toward the open doorway and lifting her skirts above her satin slippered shoes, darted toward the stairs, half expecting the music to stop.

It didn't. The duc played.

Skidding out of the room, she turned and seeing the massive staircase, hurried toward it and up the mahogany stairs.

The piano still played.

She darted right and counted out each door of one, two, three, four and…five.

The piano still played.

She drew in a breath and knocked. The piano stilled right along with her heart. In the distance, she heard a hall clock chime twelve times.

It was destiny calling.

LESSON TWELVE

Here come the stars. Earn them.

-The School of Gallantry

A muffled knock resounded in the room.

Konstantin tossed the book he'd been reading onto the bed where he lounged, rolled over and grabbed his pocket watch from the nightstand. He flicked the lid open and paused, realizing it was exactly midnight. Jesus. He set his pocket watch back onto the night stand and glanced toward the bedchamber door. Between all the servants and the duc, he could never get any time alone to even think. Not even at midnight.

Not that he was complaining.

"You may enter," he grudgingly called out in English, sitting up. "I am still awake."

The door slowly edged open and a tall, womanly figure in a bountiful evening gown lingered in the shadows, the hallway beyond much too dark to unveil a face.

He scrambled off the bed, re-tying his robe around his nudity realizing there was a woman standing in the doorway.

Konstantin blinked in disbelief as the shadow stepped forth with determined grace and poise into his room. The golden glow of candlelight revealed the pale face of a woman he'd dreamed about since leaving Russia.

His heart skidded and he almost choked.

It was Cecilia.

Only…a more provocative and dazzling version of her.

By God. She had come to him. At midnight.

Her thick, dark hair had been perfectly swept up into an elegant top knot which had silk ribbons intricately woven through its lush strands. Her pale throat, ears and wrists were showcased by large emeralds that gleamed against the candlelight of the room. And the gown she wore was a stunning golden gown that made that curvaceous body look as if the silk had been painted on in strokes across her shoulders and her waist.

Her dark eyes met his from the other side of the room and softened.

He stiffened and stupidly returned her stare.

She searched his face, lingering on his hair and then the rest of him. "I scarcely recognize you. You look so different."

For some reason, it didn't sound like a compliment. He ran a trembling hand across his face. "I…uh…I shaved and I cut my hair." He dropped his hand to his side, feeling heavy all over.

"You look incredibly handsome."

How he remained standing was beyond his comprehension. "How did you find me?"

She firmly shut the paneled door with the heel of her delicate satin slipper. "You left an address with my son."

A breath escaped him. He didn't think she would want to see him again. He had thought it was over.

She hesitated and with a slight tremor of her lips softly announced, "No babe."

His stomach flipped at the mention of a babe. He really hadn't expected those to be the first words from her lips. A part him was somewhat disappointed there was no babe. Which was idiotic really. He wasn't ready to be a father at her expense. "Thank you for telling me." The words were rote. He needed them to be, lest emotion break him.

A faint line of worry appeared between her brows. "Our last moments together should have been different."

He adjusted his robe to keep his hands steady. "I agree."

She hesitated. "I took advantage of you, Konstantin. I belittled you by proposing something unworthy of you because I was selfishly trying to keep you in my life in the only way I knew how. Do you forgive me?"

He swallowed back the ache building within him. "There is no need to apologize."

"When you left the way you did, I knew I had wronged you. I...you were very angry with me, weren't you?"

"No. I was not." He smiled brokenly, still in disbelief that she was standing before him. "Far from it. I left because it was the right thing to do for you and your girls. I did not want their good names exposed to harm given how young they are. I did it for you."

Her lips parted. "So you left that night without a word because...?" A breath escaped her as if she were in awe. She finished closing the space between them, the primrose skirts of her flowing evening gown whispering around her slow movements. She paused before him.

A new scent, one of delicate lilacs bloomed around him, heightening his awareness of her body and its heat. He liked it. A lot. He wet his lips and blurted the first thing that came to mind. "You are wearing a different perfume from the one you wore in Russia. I like it."

"I was hoping you would."

They lingered, barely a step away from each other.

She embraced him, her hands clinging to his waist before jumping to his back. Tucking her head against his chest, she said, "I wasn't ready to say it before but I am ready to say it now. I want to get to know you beyond the two days we spent in each other's arms. I want to get to know you in a respectable manner. Is that possible?"

He momentarily closed his eyes, savoring her embrace which he missed so much. He dug his fingers into her soft hair, trying to keep his hands from trembling. Knowing he shouldn't hold her for much longer, he stepped back and away, pulling himself out of her arms. Re-opening his eyes, he took in a calming breath, trying to keep his mind steady. "Cecilia. I did a lot of things in my life that I will never be able to even tell you about. I used to hurt people. Physically. You do know that, yes?"

Her features flickered. "But you don't hurt people anymore. You are not that man anymore." She tilted her chin upward, so as to better observe him, her eyes unreadable. "Would I be standing here if I believed you unworthy of a chance to be part of our lives? If anything, I proved I was unworthy of *you* by letting you go."

He didn't need this. He had just learned how to breathe without thinking about her and their nights in Russia. And now she wanted him to be a father to all three of her girls and whatever other children would come of them being together?

Wanting that responsibility was one thing.

Doing it justice was quite the other.

He strode around her, chanting to himself to remain calm and made his way toward the door and opened it. He was determined to do right by her. Determined.

He gripped the handle of the door. "I ask that you give yourself time to think about what you are saying. If you are saying these things because you feel the need to do right by me, know that I am well, Cecilia. I am forging a life for myself and am buying a home next week. It overlooks the park and will prove peaceful. The duc promised to provide formal introductions to men and women of my standing. The *nouveau riche,* as they are called. I will be accepted by these men and women for what I am. It is a good path for me to take."

She turned, tears streaking her eyes. "Have you already moved on?"

The raw hurt in her voice and the tears that streaked those beautiful eyes punched him in the gut. It was like she felt for him what he felt for her. A genuine connection and passion. He swallowed. "No. I have not moved on. How...how can I? I simply..." He opened the door wider, trying not to look at her. "Please. Let me do this for you. You do not want or need a man who used to protect all the wrong people."

"Konstantin—"

"*Please let me do the right thing.*" His voice was ragged. "Think about your daughters."

She drifted toward him. "I am ready for a new husband and my girls are ready for a new father."

"Cecilia—"

"I want you to show my girls what a good man ought to be before they go out into the world and find men of their own. Please say you will call on me tomorrow afternoon. Please. It can be a short visit. Juliet, Giselle and Abigail ardently wish to meet you. You can decide then."

Her daughters knew about him? She had told them about him. Him. As if he were worth knowing. He envisioned youthful faces gathering around him and eagerly beaming up at him as if he worth the glory of their attention. Despite his past.

Cecilia lingered before him and the open door. "We don't have to stay in London. In fact, I do not wish to stay and allow any of us to be subjected to the cruelty of a circle that does not understand genuine people. Let us go to Paris and then back to Russia as a family. Why not show my girls the city you grew up in? It could be a beautiful adventure for all of us."

Konstantin's pulse quickened. "You would move your entire family to Russia? For me?"

"Of course," she softly insisted.

She clearly understood that Russian society was more accepting. "Why are you doing this?"

"Because destiny demands this. Destiny has proven its existence. As you told me it would."

He searched her face, desperately needing to believe that destiny was with them, not against them. "How has it proven its existence?"

A small smile touched her lips. "My daughters and I live right next door at 30 Belgrave Square. 'Tis overwhelmingly obvious what destiny has in mind for us."

His lips parted, his hand dropping from the door he held open.

She released a steadying breath, her smile fading. "My girls have announced they are ready for the transition and would like to meet you based off of my affection for you. Would you be willing to agree to a courtship with a possibility toward matrimony if we find we are match?"

He dragged in an astounded breath. She wasn't just asking

to get to know him. She was asking him to be part of her life. "You are asking *me* to court *you*?"

"Yes." She stepped closer. "What is your reply, Mr. Levin?"

He focused hard on pinning his attention to her face. It was the only way he was going to remain calm. This was a moment money could never buy. It was a moment that made him feel like a man. Not a criminal who had stolen a woman's heart but a real man who had won the affections of a real woman by…being himself.

He adjusted the belt of his robe, feeling awkward. "I, uh…I am without words. Truly. When I am properly dressed and-and…*ready*, I will call on you tomorrow afternoon. I have some errands to oversee." Flowers and a ring. He needed a ring. "Expect me at three."

She hesitated. "So there is no reply?"

He smiled, unable to hold it back. "Tomorrow afternoon I will deliver a reply."

"Drat you for making me wait." She sighed. "I suppose I won't die."

Her voice clearly indicated she might.

She fingered the pearl button on the inside of her glove and eventually offered, "It appears our respectable fifteen minutes are up. I wish you a good-evening, Mr. Levin. I will see you at three tomorrow afternoon." She smiled rather superficially, turned and swept quietly down the corridor.

Something told him the woman had been waiting for a kiss. Not just an answer. Which meant, he should do this the way *he* envisioned. Not the way her circle envisioned.

"Cecilia," he called out, quickly walking toward her.

She paused and turned, her dark eyes capturing his.

He finished walking toward her and jerked to a halt before her, unable to breathe.

They stared at each other, the corridor pulsing and shrinking to a pinpoint.

"My answer is yes," he unabashedly announced.

Her lips parted. "Truly?"

"Truly." He grabbed her waist and yanked her against himself, dragging his hands down the curves of her body. "Now stay an hour. Stay an hour so I can strip you naked and keep telling you yes."

Her gloved hands jumped up to his face. "If I stay an hour," she whispered, "do you promise to still come over tomorrow at three?"

"With flowers and a ring," he whispered back. "I promise."

She grabbed the lapels of his robe and yanked him down toward herself and to his astonishment, tongued him, angling her mouth harder against his own.

He melted against her and feverishly tongued her back.

Their hands were suddenly everywhere, desperately looking for skin to touch.

They stumbled and fell against the nearest wall, kissing and kissing.

He frantically undid his robe in between ragged breaths, revealing his nudity and a more than ready cock. He slid down the length of her body, until he was on his knees before her and jerked up her skirts. Holding the fabric away from his head, he tugged up her chemise. Finally finding her through the sea of fabric, he leaned in, spreading her thighs open and sucked her wet nub.

She staggered against the wall and started sliding down. "Maybe we should...go back into the...*room*," she choked out. "Maybe we should…"

He suckled that nub until she could no longer speak and her body trembled against every flick of his tongue. She dug her hands into his hair and slid further down the wall until they were both on the floor and she was beneath him, her hair spilling out of its pins in a cascade.

He flicked his tongue faster.

"Konstantin," she panted. "I…oh God!" She held his head tighter against her lower half and writhed.

His mouth finally released her nub. "Hold onto it. Not yet." Moving her head away from the wall, he shoved her gown further above her waist, letting the curtain of fabric fall over to the side of them and grabbing a hold of each leg, he wrapped her legs around his waist.

He drove his length deep into her wetness and choked back, "I am taking you in the corridor where you—" He rolled his hips into her "—proposed to me."

She clung to him in between gasps.

He rode her into the floor faster, his body desperate for release. "I thought about you every day," he rasped against her throat.

"I thought about you every hour," she rasped back.

He savagely pounded into her, ensuring she felt every moment of his jarring movements. Their moans mingled and grew progressively louder and louder. The rapid thuds of their bodies against the floor echoed as the air grew so unbearably hot. He grunted into her, no longer able to think. He could only *feel* between uneven, ragged breaths.

She cried out, gripping his shoulders hard.

He cried out, in turn, and let all of his pleasure spiral into one long guttural shout he couldn't hold. He spilled everything into her, his core and his entire body shuddering and pulsing. He pressed himself against her, catching his breaths.

"Cecilia." He cradled her, still in disbelief that she was back in his life and in his arms.

The movement of a shadow from down the corridor made him freeze.

The duc pushed away from the far wall he was leaning against in the shadows outside the candlelight, then turned and walked in the opposite direction, the swaying ribbon of the mask dangling from his hand. He disappeared into a room and closed the door.

Konstantin swallowed, knowing the man had been watching them. Jesus Christ. He was going to bloody cut the man's heart out. Coming upon them accidentally and making a dash was one thing. Staying to leisurely watch was quite another.

Konstantin quickly pulled out of Cecilia and scrambled to yank her skirts back down, while arranging his own robe. He probably shouldn't tell Cecilia. He skimmed her beautiful face with quaking hands, trying to focus on her and only her.

Her hands slid up his robed shoulders. "I adore you."

He smiled. "And I you." He grabbed Cecilia's face and kissed her hard before releasing her lips and whispering, "I need you to go. 'Tis late. I will call on you tomorrow at three. I cannot wait to meet your girls."

She kissed his lips one last time. "We will be waiting."

He pushed himself up off the floor, ensuring his robe was in place and reached down and swept her back onto her feet. He steadied her and smoothed back long curls that had fallen from its pins. "Did you get dressed up for me?"

She smiled and eased away. "I think you know the answer to that. I had better go, Mr. Levin. Before I stay." She blew him a kiss with a pucker of full lips.

He grabbed at the air before him and fisting the imaginary kiss she bestowed him, he thudded it against his chest. "I will keep it here. Always. Let me know when you want it back."

Her smile broadened as she searched his face. "Don't ever give it back. It's yours." Gathering her skirts, she glanced back at him one last time and disappeared down the main stairwell.

When everything had grown quiet and he knew she was gone, Konstantin let out a riled breath, adjusted the belt on his robe and stalked straight toward the duc's bedchamber that was down a few doors. He wasn't letting this flit over his shoulder. If the man could openly watch him and Cecilia have sex, the man was capable of anything.

Coming to a quick halt before the closed door, Konstantin used his bare foot to bang against the door. "*Andelot*?" The son of a bitch. "Open this door!"

Several drawers slammed shut and the door swung open.

The mask was back on. It was crooked. The holes barely aligned.

Konstantin wanted to smack that crooked mask off that face. "How long were you standing against that wall watching us?" he demanded.

The duc leaned heavily against the frame of the door. The heavy scent of brandy clung to the air. "Long enough. Why?"

The man was drunk. But of course. "*Why*?" Konstantin echoed. "I will tell you why. Any normal man, be he slathered up with brandy or not, would have darted out of sight and given us privacy. Any normal man would *not* have stayed and taken off his mask so he could watch."

"Since when did I ever imply I was…*normal*?" Andelot sighed, blowing out a breath of brandy. "When you get to be a man my age, Levin, you find yourself…well…watching people for reasons that have nothing to do with sex. I have seen it all. What you and she did was...tame. Not at all what I like or what I would do with a woman." The duc reached out and sloppily patted him on the cheek like a father would a son, the man's signet ring nudging Konstantin's skin. "I am happy for you. If you have a son from it, name the boy after me given I was there to see it. Now let me sleep. I am still recovering from Thérèse." The duc pushed away from the door, staggering and slammed the door.

Konstantin blinked. Why the hell did he feel sorry for a man who had just watched him have sex with his future wife? There had to be something wrong with him.

"*When are you getting married*?" the duc called through the door.

That was random. "She and I are merely progressing into a courtship to ensure we are a match."

The door rattled. "To hell with courtship, boy. Courtship is...for the devil. It would only give her a chance to find someone else. You either know you want her to be the mother of all your children or you do not know. Which is it?" he slurred.

Konstantin sighed. "I suggest you sleep off the brandy."

"Sleep, sleep. Brandy, brandy. Cease being rude. You Russians are rude. I am not done speaking to you. Did I say I was done?"

Konstantin rolled his eyes. "Be sure to let me know when *you* are."

"Are you buying her a courtship ring? Is that the plan?"

Why were they talking through the door? "Yes, I intend to buy one. Tomorrow."

Heavy steps from within the room resounded and several drawers opened and then closed, some of them being slammed shut. "Levin?"

"Yes?"

"Are you still there?"

The man was beyond soused. "Yes. Yes, I am." He didn't know why he was but he was.

The door opened and the duc grabbed Konstantin's hand and deposited a small gold ring with a large garnet. "Take it. I have held onto it for…too long. Thérèse never accepted my proposal when we were younger. And given that she is engaged to another she never will."

Konstantin's heart constricted as the weight of that ring sat heavy in his hand. That garnet ring represented the man's dreams. Dreams that were not his to take. Dreams that were not his to even hold.

Grabbing that scarred hand, Konstantin pressed the ring back into it hard, closing that hand around it. He shook it and leaned in to the duc. "I appreciate your generosity, but this ring represents what is yours. Not mine, but yours. Fight for her. Win her back. I know you can."

The duc glanced up at him through his own haze. "How do you know I can?"

Konstantin shook that hand one last time in assurance. "Destiny. We Russians know these things."

3:07 p.m.

The Stone residence

Cecilia nervously glanced toward the sunlit parlor window from where she sat and arranged her lace morning gown for the third time. It was like waiting for the King to call.

Giselle, Juliet and Abigail primly sat elbow to elbow on the upholstered couch, their dark pinned curls piled in ringlets and white satin matching ribbons they had all insisted on. Whilst Juliet and Abigail both wore white dresses and white slippers, as was proper given their age,

Giselle, who sat between them, opted for a regal pale blue gown and red satin slippers.

Juliet pressed her gloved hands together tighter. "He is seven minutes late, Mama."

Giselle perused the French clock on the marble mantelpiece of the hearth that was a few feet away from where they sat. "A gentleman is supposed to be aware of the time."

Abigail picked at the fabric of her cotton gown. "I think he realized the amount of responsibility involved and left for Russia."

A breath escaped Cecilia. "Cease fussing. Just because he is a few minutes late doesn't mean he left for Russia. I'm quite certain he—"

The calling bell chimed through the corridor announcing a visitor.

They all jumped to their feet as the butler strode toward the door.

Abigail and Juliet grabbed each other's arms.

Giselle frantically smoothed her skirts.

Cecilia felt her entire face grow hot remembering what she and Konstantin had done last night against a wall and then the floor. She needed a glass of wine. Desperately.

Booted steps approached. The butler paused in the doorway and announced, "Lord Gunther is calling, Lady Stone. Are you receiving?"

Cecilia felt all of the blood leave her head. It was her cousin. The one whose father used to humiliate her parents when she and her family had been dependent on Lord Gunther's family for finances. Before Cecilia married well and ended her cousin's advances by providing her parents with everything herself. In their youth, Gunther had repeatedly tried to do more than kiss her. He eventually married and had children of his own and kept to himself, but whenever their paths crossed, she always panicked and ensured she was never alone. She didn't trust him.

Cecilia glanced toward her daughters, who gaped at her wide-eyed. They knew the story about her cousin all too well.

She set her chin. "I am not receiving anyone but Mr. Levin. Please turn him away."

"Yes, my lady." The butler inclined his head and departed to dismiss their unannounced guest.

Giselle hurried over to Cecilia and whispered, "He called several times and kept asking to see you. The governess was quite annoyed with him given he wanted to know when you would return. He hasn't associated with us before. Knowing how he used to treat you in your youth, his intentions scare me, Mama."

Cecilia let out a shaky breath knowing it. "His intentions have no bearing on us. He will be turned away every time."

A shout from the butler caused them all to pause.

Lord Gunther walked into the room, his grey satin trimmed morning coat announcing the extravagance that had always followed the man. His greying, blond hair was meticulously brushed and parted.

He'd worn his hair the same since 1808.

Hazel eyes briefly met her gaze. He inclined his head. "You look well for yourself, cousin." Turning to the girls, he smiled and lowered his shaven chin against his silk cravat. "I am certain you are all pleased to have your mother return from her travels abroad after so many months away."

Cecilia tried not to panic knowing he was in her house and talking to her girls. She grabbed up a vase from a side table and made her way toward him. "Gunther, I ask that you not speak to my girls. Get out." She held up the vase in warning.

He held out a hand toward the vase. "Please. I need to speak to you."

Cecilia felt her throat tighten, remembering all too well how her poor papa would quietly accept funds from Gunther's balding father who would casually point to items in their home and ask that it be taken in return for the funds received. And how Gunther himself, at eighteen, would corner her alone at fifteen and demand 'kisses' and other physical 'favors' as if it were his right. Merely because his father assisted in paying their debts. That was the sort of family they were. The Gunthers had always believed in making everyone crawl. Because of them, she had stupidly given up all of her dreams in her youth to pursue the wrong ones: financial ones.

The calling bell rang.

Her daughters' faces flickered in panic.

Cecilia, however, felt a lethal calm embrace her knowing it was Konstantin. It was like he was destined to be in her life to protect her and her girls. She lowered the vase and set it aside.

Running steps approached and the butler appeared again. "Mr. Levin is calling, Lady Stone. Shall I call for the footmen and escort Lord Gunther out?"

The footmen didn't have the experience Konstantin did. "No. That won't be necessary, Stanley. If Lord Gunther does not leave, Mr. Levin will escort him out."

Lord Gunther paused, his brows flickering. "Who is Mr. Levin?"

Cecilia didn't move. "A man you will regret meeting. I am *not* the fifteen-year- old girl you used to corner. Nor will I be intimidated in my own home."

His brows came together. "I know you have always thought the worst of me, and rightfully so, but I am not that boy anymore. I need to speak to you alone, Cecilia. Please."

Giselle, Juliet and Abigail rounded toward Cecilia and stood between them, announcing that they weren't leaving the room.

Cecilia stepped around them, refusing to let her girls anywhere near him. "You have long lost the privilege of my trust."

Gunther blinked rapidly. "I am calling you for reasons outside my own pride. I would not be here otherwise. I know how you despise me."

She paused, sensing his tone was genuine. "Why are you here?"

"Can I speak to you alone?" he pressed.

She shook her head, her skin crawling at remembering the way he always tried to touch her in their youth. "No."

He edged toward her. "I am not going to touch you! I am a married man. A happily married man, I assure you."

Her chest heaved. She couldn't trust him. She couldn't. "Leave."

Within moments, Konstantin strode in, wearing an expensive-looking beige morning coat and matching trousers, carrying two large wicker baskets in each grey-gloved hand. One basket was filled with orchids and the other was filled with a variety of small parcels carefully tied with bright pink ribbons. His black hair was dashingly swept back with tonic and his rugged shaven face as cheerful as his green eyes were well-amused and bright.

He paused at seeing Lord Gunther, his features tightening. He eyed the girls and then Cecilia. "Is everything all right?" His voice indicated he knew it wasn't.

Cecilia almost felt faint at seeing him. "Mr. Levin, would you please escort Lord Gunther out? He is not welcome here." Her voice trembled, despite her trying to remain calm. She couldn't help it. There were too many years of angst buried within her. Every time she saw Gunther, she saw herself at fifteen, shoving away unwanted hands.

Konstantin slowly set both baskets he was holding onto the floor, his demeanor and gaze darkening. He straightened to his full height. "Lord Gunther. I ask that you follow me out."

Gunther turned toward Konstantin. "I only wish to speak to her."

Konstantin removed his coat and tossed it to the floor, his gaze never once leaving her cousin. "We are taking this outside." His voice was ragged.

Oh, Lord. Cecilia held out a quick hand, realizing Konstantin intended to fight him. "No, Konstantin. Don't hurt him. He isn't worth your good name. I just want him to leave."

Konstantin shifted his jaw. "If that is what you want." He stalked toward Gunther. "You heard her. You need to leave. Now."

Gunther edged back and held up both hands. He slowly rounded Konstantin and made his way toward the door of the receiving room. He paused and turned back to Cecilia. Letting out a long breath, he finally said, "I need two thousand pounds. Or my wife and children go with me to debtor's prison. I care nothing about myself, but I cannot have them reduced to such a hardship. I have sold everything I could. I would not have come here but my wife insisted given your vast donations to charities that you would show us kindness."

Cecilia swallowed. She had met the man's wife once. A quiet woman who smiled at everything. Although she despised Gunther, and nothing would ever change that, she was not about to punish the woman or Gunther's children for it. "I will ensure your debts are paid in full. All I ask is that you not call on me again."

Gunther searched her face, his eyes suddenly streaked with tears. "I regret hurting you. I really do. I was young and didn't know how to go about showing my affection. I'm sorry. Truly. It is not who I am anymore.

It isn't."

It was the only apology she had *ever* received from him. And it was enough. "I will send the money to your wife. It will be delivered into her hands."

Konstantin made his way to Gunther. "I will pay for it."

Cecilia almost cried.

Gunther sniffed. "Thank you for showing kindness, cousin. I...thank you." He disappeared down the corridor.

Konstantin disappeared after him.

Cecilia held her breath, trying to listen. Low voices were exchanged but nothing more.

The door eventually closed and Konstantin re-appeared. He held Cecilia's gaze for a moment. "He knows not to call on you again."

She half-nodded.

Coming up to her, he quickly tugged her toward himself, setting her head against his chest with a large gloved hand. "Are you all right?" he asked against her hair. "Please tell me you are."

Letting out a long breath, she leaned against him heavily and pushed away all thoughts of her cousin. She wasn't about to let anything take this moment away from her. A moment of knowing that this man, this beautiful man was hers. All hers. "Yes," she murmured against him. "Thank you."

"Was he the cousin you told me about in Russia?"

He remembered. "Yes." She pulled away from his embrace and forced a smile. "He appears to be a different man. Which I am glad for." She turned and gestured toward her three girls who lingered in stunned silence. "Konstantin, I would like for you to meet Abigail, Juliet and Giselle. John sends his apologies for not being here. He had some estate business to tend to but promised to join us at supper which I am inviting you to. Can you join us at seven o'clock tonight?"

Konstantin nodded. "I will be there." He walked to the doorway and swiped up the two baskets he had earlier set aside. Turning back, he came to a halt before her girls, his gaze jumping from face to face. "Saint Peter. They all look like you, Cecilia. Every last one of them."

A much needed laugh escaped Cecilia. "The poor things."

Giselle set her chin. "You handled Lord Gunther beautifully, Mr. Levin. I was impressed you didn't feel the need to showcase your fists."

Konstantin sighed. "I have showcased them enough in my life."

Juliet bit her lip and peered toward the large basket filled with parcels. "Is that for us?"

Abigail kicked out a foot toward Juliet. "Cease being rude. We almost lost our lives and all you can think of is whether those parcels are for us?"

Konstantin smiled, held out the basket filled with well over ten small parcels and leaned toward them, lowering his voice. "These are actually all for you. It is the reason why I am late."

Juliet side-glanced at her sister.

Konstantin held out the basket and waggled its weight playfully toward each of them. "Would one of you ladies care to take this basket so I can deliver the orchids to your mother?"

Juliet popped out her arms. "I will take it!"

"Yes, thank you!" Abigail and Giselle chimed in unison.

All three hurriedly took the basket and set it on the couch. Turning their backs to Mr. Levin, they commenced rummaging through it, excitedly pointing out that their names were on them.

Konstantin swiveled on his booted heel toward Cecilia and quirked a brow, holding up the basket of orchids. "Are you supposed to come over here? Or am I supposed to come over there? How do respectable people do this?"

Cecilia felt as if she might burst knowing this man was hers. She gathered her skirts and swept toward him, trying to create the illusion she was as regal as he made her feel. "Respectable people always meet halfway, Mr. Levin."

He held her gaze and rounded toward her.

They paused before each other.

He slowly turned the basket toward her, revealing an oval emerald ring carefully strung to one of the center orchids. He intently searched her face. "I tried to match the color of the emerald set you wore last night."

Cecilia pressed a hand to her throat and leaned in. "Konstantin. It's beautiful."

The girls paused and frantically abandoned their gifts. One by one, they gathered around them, peering at the orchid display and the ring.

Konstantin leaned in, setting his shaven chin on the handle of the basket. "We have an audience."

She smiled. "I noticed." She reached out and delicately unbound the satin ribbon strung to the white orchid. She slipped the ring from the ribbon and held out the ring to her daughters so they could all admire the glint of the oval emerald. It was cut beautifully.

Cecilia breathed out, "I can't believe this is happening."

He leaned in and softly said, "If you feel your knees getting weak, let me know."

Her knees wobbled. "They feel weak."

All three girls and Konstantin grabbed for her.

She let out a laugh. "They don't feel *that* weak."

Konstantin set down the basket at their feet. Taking the ring and her left hand, he lowered both so everyone could see and slipped the ring onto her finger. Glancing toward each of the girls, he asked, "May I have your permission, ladies, to court this amazing woman until she is ready to honor me with more?"

Cecilia swallowed. He wasn't asking her. He was asking her girls.

Abigail and Juliet beamed up at Konstantin as Giselle gushed, "We would be honored, Mr. Levin. All we ask is that you make her smile every day."

Overwhelmed, a tear unexpectedly spilled forth, trailing down her cheek.

Konstantin paused. His voice softened. "Cecilia."

Everyone looked at her.

She frantically brushed away the tear. "'Tis happiness, I assure you."

Konstantin edged toward her and grabbed both of her hands, squeezing them hard.

Cecilia felt as if her girls were meeting the father they should have had all along.

EPILOGUE

Embrace your new life knowing you have earned it.

-The School of Gallantry

A year and a half later

Saint Petersburg, Russia

Cecilia smoothed the pudgy cheek of little Gérard who was looking up at her with green eyes and babbling, "Da, da, da." She kissed his small head of soft, curling dark hair and switched him to her other hip, adjusting his white cotton ensemble.

They were going to be late.

She quickly rounded the last corner of the lavish house Konstantin had bought for them that overlooked the Neva River, and followed the giggling voices of her girls. She eventually found Giselle, Juliet and Abigail gathered around Konstantin.

Konstantin was leisurely stretched out on a chaise lounge with his leather boots crossed over his ankles. He angled a Russian leather-bound book toward himself and casually announced in English, "That was rather good, Juliet. Now Giselle, I ask that you say something about the Emperor in Russian."

Giselle smoothed her pale blue gown, glanced up toward the ceiling and pertly recited in broken Russian, "The Emperor is very well known for...*passing* idiotic laws that ought to be...*castrated*."

Konstantin snorted and scrambled to sit up on the chaise, saying in English, "Whilst that was incredibly good, Giselle, and I do mean that, the last word was supposed to be *eliminated*. Not *castrated*. Never use the word castration around Russian men. Unless you want them to panic."

Cecilia let out a laugh. Bless the man's daily lessons with the girls. "I hate to interrupt yet another marvelous lesson, but we are late for our picnic out in the country. Two of our Russian neighbors will be joining us and therefore we cannot be rude and let them wait. The carriage and our food and baskets have already been sitting for well over twenty minutes."

Abigail and Juliet jumped up. Grabbing at each other's arms, to keep the other from getting ahead, they darted out of the room, slippered feet scrambling.

In between the scrambling, Juliet announced, "This time, I get the seat by Papa."

Abigail argued back. "But you always sit by Papa."

"That is because I am his favorite."

"You are *not*."

Cecilia bit back a smile and called out, "Cease needlessly arguing. There are no favorites in this house!"

"Quite right, Mama. Quite right." Giselle stood and sashayed past Cecilia in the only way an almost eighteen-year-old could. "Did you hear me speak? I am really quite good. My Russian is getting so good, in fact, I'll be able to marry any Russian man I want."

Cecilia rolled her eyes and gestured toward the door. "In the meantime, we have a picnic. Try not to be late."

Giselle giggled, bit her lip, gathered her skirts and darted out of the room.

Cecilia turned toward Konstantin and sighed. "The day hasn't even started and yet I am exhausted. Thoroughly exhausted."

Konstantin tossed the book he was holding onto the chaise and jumped to his feet. Adjusting his grey morning coat, he strode over. "And yet you keep asking me for another babe? I keep telling you, it is not wise for us to be trying so soon. It has only been six months."

"I am past forty," she argued. "If we don't have the last one now, it will never happen."

"I can assure you, it will happen. All we have to do is try at midnight and you are done."

She snorted. "Midnight can only help a woman my age so much."

"Ba, ba...*ba*," Gérard offered, waving about a frantic hand.

Konstantin grinned and reached out and took Gérard from her arms, nuzzling the boy's head. "Yes. Exactly. You tell her. You tell her I refuse to exhaust her."

Cecilia stood up on toes and kissed Konstantin's cheek soundly. "Can we not try for another babe? *Please*? I am done waiting. You are being needlessly stubborn."

Using Gérard's pudgy little hand, Konstantin pointed at her accusingly. "You are not listening to what I said."

She sighed, knowing there was no use arguing with him about it. Drat him. "We have to go. The girls are waiting."

"Are you angry with me?"

"A little."

"I cannot have that. Come here." He leaned down captured her lips, lingering.

She closed her eyes, melting into that kiss in the way she always did.

A small hand frantically patted its way toward her breast and tugged on her décolletage.

A bubble of a laugh escaped her as she broke away and re-opened her eyes. Whilst she was glad she didn't hire a wet nurse, as ladies in her circle always did, the duty of feeding sometimes came at the most inconvenient times. "Apparently, Gérard is hungry." She wagged her hands toward him. "Give him here. I will feed him before we leave."

Konstantin glanced down at their boy and tsked. "So much for our picnic. He is making his own." Depositing Gérard into her arms, he searched her face. "You have not had *your* Russian lesson today."

"You know how utterly hopeless I am at Russian. I try but nothing ever comes of it."

"That is because you are not practicing. *Vot moe serdtse. Ono polno lubvi.*" He searched her face again. "Now translate."

She quirked a brow. "I never heard that one before. How can I translate?"

He shifted toward her. "*Here is my heart. It is full of love.*" He smiled boyishly. "Now say it back to me in Russian."

She rolled her eyes. "I can't even remember the first word. But I do love you. In case you were wondering."

"I was wondering. And I genuinely think more lessons are in order."

She laughed. "I look forward to learning the entire Russian alphabet. But in the meantime, tell the girls I need a few minutes to feed Gérard. Now off with you."

He smiled, inclined his head and adjusted his coat, striding toward the doorway. Pulling out his watch, he checked the time and paused. His smile faded.

She seated herself in a chair and unpinned the front of her gown, letting Gérard latch onto her breast. "What is it?"

He glanced back at her, his green eyes capturing hers. He wagged the watch at her, rattling the silver chain attached to his pocket. "My watch ceased ticking. Again. It stopped at the hour of twelve. Again. It never wants to go past the hour."

She glanced up. "Did you not have it fixed by a clockmaker a week ago?"

"Yes. That makes for nine times I have taken it in the past few weeks. *Nine.*"

She cradled Gérard. "It is rather old. I suggest you retire Miss Bane's watch into a glass case we can display it as a family heirloom."

"I think I will have to." After a long moment, he turned back toward her and observed her feeding Gérard. He eventually said, "I think Miss Bane is telling us it's time for another baby. What do you think?"

Wonders never ceased. He was finally saying yes to another baby.

1/14

DATE DUE

Made in the USA
Lexington, KY
17 January 2014